THE FORGIVENESS FILES

Toria Newman

TJI
Toria's Journey International

Cover Design & Photography: Jan Kaluza   (jankaluza.net)

ISBN: Softcover   978-0-473-65383-5
          Epub   978-0-473-65384-2

Additional copies of this book can be ordered from online bookstores worldwide or directly from the author in NZ (NZ customers only), whose contact information appears in the back of this book.
A catalogue record for this book is available from the National Library of New Zealand.

Edited & Published: WordWyze Publishing
WordWyze.nz

ACKNOWLEDGEMENTS

Dr Hoy

I would like to thank Dr Ben Hoy for saving my sight. I will be forever filled with gratitude and amazed that I can see all the beautiful colours and special things that make me happy. Dr Hoy had an assistant called Reed. This young man helped me to feel relaxed and gave me the confidence to try to extend myself so that I could allow the staff to do particular tests that were difficult because of my disability. Thanks, guys.

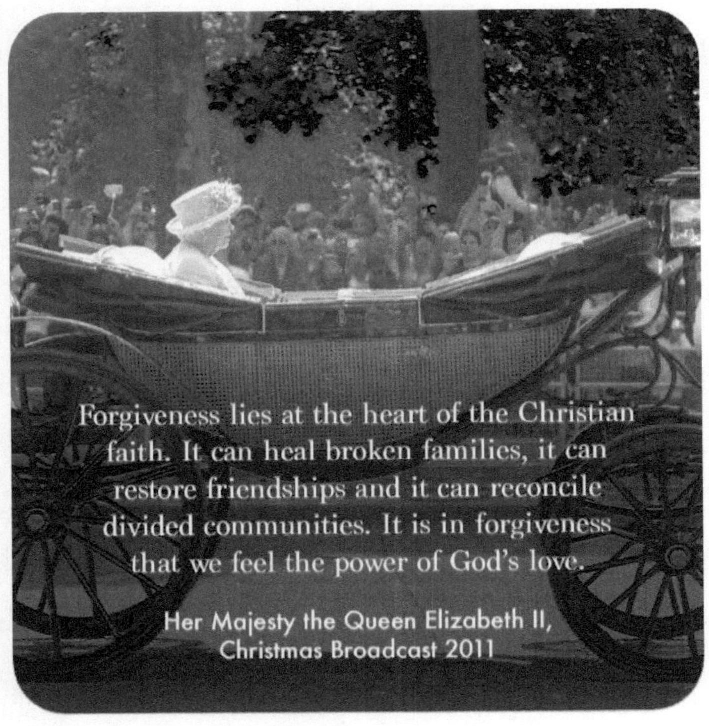

ENDORSEMENTS

Elevate CDT (Christian Disability Trust)

We at Elevate are so grateful to the Lord for His Grace and Provision and for all our people who have been involved. The Ministry began over 40 years ago, and during that time, the vision has become clear and prospered to where it is today. We started small with meetings. Then as we developed, grew and matured, we expanded to have camps and seminars around the nation and also overseas.

So, we have CFFD (Christian Fellowship for Disabled). This is mainly for people with physical disabilities. There are now branches all over New Zealand and a branch in the Philippines. One branch that was started in Fiji is now a church! Joy Ministries is mainly for people who have intellectual disabilities. Emmanuel is for families where there are children with disabilities. Torch is for the Blind and Visually impaired. Then there is the Drop-In Centre and main office in Auckland, New Zealand.

Our Magazine started very small. At first, it was only two sides of a page. Today, it is a thriving publication of sixteen sides. It is printed in full colour and is sent all over New Zealand and the world. The magazine is called the Encourager and has testimonies and events that inspire the reader. We have also printed many other helpful leaflets, booklets and books.

Our main thrust in Elevate is to touch people with the Gospel and to encourage them in their faith and walk with Jesus. We also stand beside and motivate our folk to reach their full potential.

We have DAS (Disability Awareness Sunday) in June or whenever it suits the Church. This is where our folk take part in Church Services. In this way, we teach that people with disabilities should be part of the body of Christ, to be included, valued, accepted and encouraged to use their God-given talents. We look to the Lord to show us where Elevate can be best used in the future.

Margie Willers, who is severely disabled due to Cerebral Palsy, is a dynamic speaker and writer of several books. Margie's first book, *Awaiting the Healer*, was a CBA Silver Award winner in 1992. Her second book was called *Undaunted Faith*, published by Castle Ltd, New Zealand. For many years, Margie travelled throughout New Zealand as a motivational speaker, sharing her story and teaching students as they prepared for their own God-ordained journey. Margie is a great inspiration to all of us who know her personally and those who have heard her testimony.

Toria Newman has also been involved with Elevate, Christian Disabilities Trust since the early days. She says that Elevate has an essential place in the community. The meetings and camps provide companionship, biblical teaching on life skills, and spiritual and emotional care often unavailable elsewhere. Regarding her God-given Ministry, Toria believes that as a disabled person, she is uniquely positioned to stand beside and support others who find daily living challenging. In her own way, she endeavours to encourage them to find their own unique place in the world and then step out so that they can pursue their dreams and do great things.

INSPIRATION FOR THIS BOOK.

The character of Eli Evans is based on Lance Wallnau. He makes me smile. I enjoy watching his nightly video chats that he does from his home. He appears to have a large library that is intriguing.

Lance Wallnau is a strategist, futurist and sought-after motivational communicator. Based in Dallas, Texas, he directs the Lance Learning Group, teaching, shaping and offering ongoing consultation to companies needing to expand their knowledge and increase their market share.

PROLOGUE

Hi everyone, Robbie here.

This story, *The Forgiveness Files*, is very special to me. The events cover only seven days, but in that short time, a lot happens. As it goes, it is not just one single story. I meet many new people who teach me important things that help to change my life forever.

Yes, I am blessed to have been given an inquiring mind and a crazy sense of humour that helps me to portray the people in my world and their stories. They are sometimes heart-breaking, a timely reminder that life is incredibly difficult for some. At other times, the stories are full of happiness, with ongoing development, overcoming obstacles and victory. This is why our Creator has given us His compassion, the ability to reach out and impart His healing love to the discouraged and broken-hearted.

Finally, the stories provide a unique window into Heaven, a peek beyond our earthly life, into our future. Many people don't believe that there is such a place. Yet many others who also have had near-death experiences will affirm that there is because they have been there. My heartfelt desire is that this book will encourage provoking and thoughtful conversations that bring faith and hope.

This is the third book in the story of Robbie's life. You can read about more of Robbie's adventures in the other two books, *The Chrysalis* and *Undercover: Miss Speedy Wheels*.

CHAPTER ONE

It was mid-March 2019. The year had begun with such promise. As yet, there had been no great disasters in my world. Well, none that would affect me personally. The weather was still very warm, although sometimes I could feel a slight hint of a chill in the air, indicating that Winter was in my near future. Everything seemed to be as it should be. Then came Thursday. I will never forget. Yes, it was definitely a Thursday. On this day, a series of events would happen that would change my life forever.

BANG! THUMP! CRASH! PING!

What?! What?! The streaming sunlight stung my eyes as I was jolted awake by the noise. Quickly, I tried to focus and centre my mind on what I could hear somewhere in the distance. Could something be going on in the kitchen? *I must go and check it out*, was my next thought. Gingerly, I pushed the blankets off my tired body, slipped out of bed, hopped into my electric wheelchair and scooted down the hallway. By now, I could hear Mom and Dad talking. They seemed to be having a serious discussion about something that had just happened. I could tell that Mom was stressed. She had regressed into her Bette Davis mode, where everything she did and said was in a very pronounced tone. Again, I heard the crash-bang sound of utensils being thrown this way and that. It was like she was performing the final act of the dying swan to an audience of thousands. This was comical to watch in the short term, especially when she wanted to impress someone. However, if she was angry or just in a foul mood, look out! I knew from times past that I should be careful. I should not complain or make any sort of smart comment. If I did, I would not get breakfast and be sent straight back to my bedroom to reflect on my bad behaviour. Dad also ignored this peculiar manner of hers. He didn't seem to be in the best mood to deal with her right now, either. The atmosphere just didn't seem right this morning. Perhaps I should inquire further.

"What's wrong?" I asked my father. "Why are you two up so early? Has something bad happened?"

"Your sister is coming home," replied Dad. "I'm picking her up from the bus in about half an hour. Yes, it seems that something terrible has happened to Angela. And it sounds like it is to do with her boyfriend. Your mother can fill you in with the details." Then he left to go and get dressed.

I looked over at Mom. She was scrubbing the kitchen bench tops so ferociously that I thought she might put a hole in them. Yet she didn't speak. She was so preoccupied with the problem concerning Angela that I don't think she was even aware I was in the room. So, I would wait until she was ready and able to tell me what she knew.

Angela is thirty years old this August, eighteen months older than me. She first left home when she was sixteen. Moving to Auckland, she thought she would study to earn a nursing degree. But she found life difficult there, unable to find a job to support herself and became homeless. Living on the streets, she fell into the wrong crowd and began taking drugs. When Dad got wind of it, he went to Auckland, found her and brought her home. Even though we live in a small town, we have some excellent services here. Angela went to stay with another family and received drug and alcohol counselling. It worked for her. She cleaned up her act and moved to Wellington. There, she was able to fulfil her dream of training to be a nurse. So, I wondered what had happened now. Could she be back on the drugs? She and I are not close these days. But I was sure that, had there been a problem, Mom or Dad would have mentioned it. No, this must be something new.

Just then, Uncle Edgar appeared at the kitchen door. He was in his long johns, a long-sleeved undershirt and his hair, such as he had, was sticking up every which way. Oh, and he wasn't wearing his false teeth. He looked hilarious.

"What's going on?" he asked Mom, echoing my own question. "Why is everyone up so early? A man needs his beauty sleep, you know."

I almost laughed out loud, recalling the morning he arrived. It had been 5 am, and he banged and banged on the door until Dad answered it. But today, he was indignant because others had disturbed his sleep.

"Sit down, Edgar, and I'll cook you breakfast," said Mom. His voice seemed to return Mom's mind to the present, and she pulled the saucepan out of the cupboard. "Bacon and eggs on toast?"

Uncle Edgar's eyes lit up like a Christmas tree. Quickly, he sat down, happy and eager, his mouth salivating at the mere thought of it. No, he would not be complaining anymore today. I also took the opportunity to line up for mine. I don't eat bacon, not because I don't like it. I just find that fried bacon is too hard for me to chew and difficult to swallow. Eggs are great, preferably scrambled. Down the hatch, and they are gone.

Dad had been away for about twenty minutes when we heard his car pull up in the driveway. The front door opened, and he walked in, followed by Angela. Mom walked over to her and gave her a long and tender hug. She whispered her welcome home and assured her that everything would be okay. Dad took her suitcase to her room. Then he came back to join us. Now that Angela was sitting across from me, I took the time to study her. She appeared very pale, and her clothes and hair looked quite dishevelled. It seemed to me that she had just jumped out of bed, packed her bag and ran. More obvious was the black eye and bruised cheek, not to mention her badly cut lip. There was a great deal here that I didn't yet know. Perhaps I hadn't heard the details, but I could read the evidence. Somebody had done these things to her. And they had been brutal.

"Angela is going to be staying for a while," said Dad. "We are going to give her some space and time to heal. If she wants to tell us what has happened to her, she will, in her own time."

We all nodded our understanding and continued eating. Angela didn't speak at all. She just sat there, playing with her food, pushing it this way and that. I could tell that she had a great deal on her mind. The minutes passed, yet there was still no conversation from her. She looked very withdrawn and unaware of what was happening around her. This was very sad to see. Everyone was on edge as we all observed her body language, but none of us knew quite what to do. At that moment, a driver tooted his car horn as he passed our house. It wasn't a loud noise, but it must have resonated with Angela. Suddenly, she jumped up, making a single cry, and ran to the corner of the room. Standing for just one moment, she slid down the wall, crumpled to the floor and crouched there. I watched as she sat, whimpering and shaking like a leaf, her arms covering her head. She seemed terrified of something, or maybe someone. Mom ran to her and held her close, trying to calm her. Then they both stood up, and Mom walked her to the bedroom.

I looked over at Dad. He was visibly distressed. Yes, it was true that Angela had been a handful in the past. But she had never acted this way before. Her confident, outgoing attitude was no longer there. This was an Angela I didn't know. In fact, I had never seen anyone act and react like this. She was just a shell of her former self, making me afraid. Many questions flooded my mind. Who had done this to Angela? Was it the boyfriend? Will she ever recover? How will she cope in the future? Of course, I am aware of the effects of domestic violence against both men and women. It is a huge problem in today's world. I am pleased, though, that in Angela's case, no children are involved. I looked to Dad for answers, but he was silent, contemplating what this may mean for us all.

Uncle Edgar sat quietly, waiting for permission to comment. Having him stay with us these past few months has given me a new appreciation and respect for him. He truly is a lovely man, thoughtful, considerate and respectful of my parents, as it is their house. A true gentleman. It seems he is happy and relaxed here, which makes me happy too.

After breakfast, I went back into my bedroom to check my emails on my digital tablet. I needed to hear from my beloved Pete right now. Thankfully, there was a message from him. I could feel every beat of his heart in each word. Suddenly, I felt calm. My fear subsided, and I was happy again. Angela's situation had rattled me and made me feel unsafe. It had brought things to the surface of my emotions that I didn't know were there. I needed to get out of the house; blow the cobwebs out of my head. I wrote a quick email to Pete, explaining the situation at home and let him know I would be in touch later. Then I got dressed and went to the kitchen where Mom was. She looked up and smiled when she saw me. To my great relief, she had come out of her strange mood and was much more relaxed. I guessed it was because Angela was home and she could take care of her.

"What's on your agenda for today?" Mom wanted to know.

"I'm going to the mall for a bit of timeout and shopping therapy. Would you like to come with me?"

"Well, I would normally," she assured me. "But I think that I ought to stay with Angela. She is in a terrible way."

"Has she said anything about what has happened to her, or who did it?"

"No," Mom sighed deeply. "She seems to be very shut up inside herself. I think she will need a lot of help to come through this one."

"Are you going to be okay if I leave for a while?" Then I laughed as I thought about what I had just said. "Come to think about it," I added. "What could I do if I stayed and something happened? Not much, eh?"

"Well, you could run over his toes." And she laughed. "I think that your father has everything in hand. He has been speaking to Mike at the police station, and I believe they will put some security measures in place for Angela."

"Good." I felt a lot better hearing this. Perhaps with Mike on the job, a visual police presence, Angela would feel safe, and we could all relax, I thought. "Do you think that the no-good boyfriend did that to her?" I enquired.

"I don't know for sure," she replied. "But that is what your father thinks."

Yes, Dad had that covered, I thought. That guy ought not to come near here. If he does, he will get a short shift. I smiled to myself. A little light relief is what I need, I decided. This seemed to be the perfect time to visit Miriam and the rabbi who lived next door. I no longer wanted to shop at the mall.

Grabbing my purse and tucking it in beside me, I headed out the door. Oooh, a sudden wintry blast hit my face so ferociously that it almost took my breath away. This was another stark reminder that the cold weather was not far away. Momentarily, I stopped to appreciate the beauty of our gardens. My mom certainly had done a stellar job designing and choosing each plant perfectly. I love roses, and so does she. I smiled as I surveyed the small corner garden that she called *Robbie's Delight*. She had made it just for me. How special! Mom has become more approachable since becoming a Christian. She and I have shared many memorable mother-daughter moments in the past eighteen months. We go shopping together, laugh over comical family stories and have great in-depth spiritual conversations. Again, I smiled as pictures of my father came to mind. So far, she hasn't convinced him to go to Church with her. He has a myriad of different excuses. The latest is that he must stay home and ensure Uncle Edgar doesn't burn the house down with his roll-your-own cigarettes. She knows, of course, that he is just stalling. And I don't understand why he won't go. He and Pastor Jon Ward are great friends. They often go fishing together. It's not as though she's asking him to go to a girlie party and buy Tupperware. Men! Who can figure them out?

Suddenly, I was aware that the atmosphere around me had changed. I now felt more relaxed. My mind was no longer centred around the sad events that had disturbed our household this morning. Yes, I was sympathetic to Angela's situation, and I did want to help in some way. However, I felt I had to take time to absorb the things I had seen and heard. So, for some time, I just sat and admired everything around me. Even though there was a chill in the air, the sun's rays gave brilliant colour to everything upon which they fell. At that moment, I felt the warmth of deep pleasure sweep through me like a grateful infusion of life-giving blood to a thirsty body. Over the fence, I could see Miriam's washing fluttering carefree in the wind. So, I gave thanks to God for bringing her into my life. She and the rabbi had become significant people in my world. I no longer spent hours sitting alone, reading fictional novels, feeling unfulfilled. The couple had opened their home and hearts to me, treating me respectfully and as an equal. My life was absolutely on the right track now, and I was happy.

Driving out the gate in my chair, I felt content. Suddenly, Benny, the cat, appeared. I stopped and bent down to greet him.

"Hello, you sweet boy," I whispered. Benny always understands me. He looked up at me and meowed his reply. As always, he eagerly smooched around my chair and readily accepted, even demanding the attention I lavished upon him. Then he jumped on my lap and lay down in quiet repose. So, I drove up the ramp and knocked at Miriam's door. She welcomed me as always, and we went into the kitchen. She quickly filled the teapot and coffee pot and brought out the cakes she had baked earlier.

"Now, Benny," she warned. "You be a good boy and stay quiet. He has been running through the house like a mad thing all morning."

"Is it a full moon?" I jokingly asked.

"I have no idea," she replied. And she looked through the oven door to check the status of the new batch of cakes that were baking. A wonderful aroma of cooking filled the room. I knew that it wouldn't be long before the rabbi appeared. I could hear two men discussing points of the Bible in another room, and how they applied to life and the political systems of today. I recognised the voice of the rabbi but not the other.

"Who is with the rabbi?" I wanted to know. Maybe it was none of my business, and perhaps I was just nosy, but the conversation sounded so interesting and enticing. I tried to eavesdrop. The two men seemed to be discussing the political situation in the tiny nation of Morgandy in the Caribbean and Israel, aligning it with things written about in the Bible. Rabbi Mirsky is a Messianic Jew and a follower of Yeshua, or Jesus, as He is more commonly known in the Christian community. So, it was not surprising that he was discussing these matters. The guy whose voice I didn't recognise seemed very knowledgeable and confident about the things he believed. His accent told me that he was perhaps from the USA. I would investigate further.

"Oh, that's Eli," Miriam giggled, and her eyebrows rose as she talked about him. "He's very excitable, especially when talking about politics and Biblical prophecy. It seems to be his passion. He writes books about it as well." She took a bite of her cake and poured three cups of tea and one cup of coffee. "He's American," she confided. "The man has no taste for tea." Then she called the two men, telling them to come and eat.

"He's not a weirdo, is he?" I whispered. "A screw loose?"

Miriam threw her head back and laughed heartily.

"You are so funny, Robbie," she said. "I love your sense of humour. No, Eli isn't a weirdo. He's just excited about all that is going on in the world today. And he enjoys discussing it and teaching about it. You can see some of his videos on the internet. Just look for Eli Evans. And he is a big fan of social media. I hear that from different friends. He often does live broadcasts. I never see them, of course, because I don't go on social media like others. But my Samuel also says that he does."

Just then, the rabbi appeared at the door with his friend Eli.

"Robbie, your policeman friends and your father just went into your house," the rabbi informed me. "Is there a problem over there?"

"My sister Angela came home this morning," I told them. "She has been badly beaten up. I think that I should go home." Yes, I was perturbed about what I had seen earlier and wanted to see what was being done about it. "I will come back later."

Miriam lifted Benny off my knee and put him in his basket in the corner of the kitchen. Everyone offered their sympathies and assured me that they were available to help wherever possible. I acknowledged Eli as I passed him. Yes, he did sound interesting. So, I hoped that he would be around at least for a few days.

Arriving home, I quickly entered the living room, where everyone was gathered. Angela sat silently in one of the easy chairs while Mom, Dad, and the two policemen, Mike and Jeff, discussed how they would keep her safe. Dressed in jeans and a T-shirt, she looked fragile and small. Many tell-tale signs of past injuries could be seen on her arms and neck. As I suspected, Angela's injuries had been caused by the no-good boyfriend. Sadly, she had stayed with him too long. Repeated beatings had left her mentally, emotionally and physically scarred, perhaps for a lifetime. I hoped not. I understand the associated problems, and it is challenging for an abused partner to break away and stay away. Some people find it tough to end the relationship permanently. They believe it is their fault; they must have done something to deserve that horrible treatment. So, time after time, they return to the relationship, thinking they can fix it. The truth is, once the cycle of violence is started, there is very little that either partner can do about it until outside help is sought.

"Hi Robbie," said Mike. "Where have you been? We didn't see you in town. Where were you hiding?" He and Jeff looked dapper in their crisp, clean policeman uniforms. But I knew that by the end of the day, Mike would not be looking that smartly dressed.

"No, I didn't go there. I was next door talking to Miriam," I informed him. "There is a guy visiting them that I have never seen before. He and the rabbi were talking about world events. Eli is his name. Miriam says that he has written books and is on the internet. I'm going to check him out."

"Good looking?" Jeff inquired. "We want some advance notice if you are planning to marry him."

"Yes," Mike concurred. "We'll need to prepare Cookie for the dreaded news. You know how emotional he can get. Who will make our lunch at the restaurant if he is too upset to cook?"

"Now, that would be a disaster," said Dad. His body shook with laughter as he entered into the banter. "I can see the news headlines now. Hungry Horse Restaurant Closed: Police Department in Disarray. You boys may just have to go on a diet."

I also noticed that Angela was looking amused. I still hadn't heard her speak yet, but I got the impression that she might be feeling better. Her shoulders and arms were somewhat more relaxed now.

"Cookie could make the wedding breakfast," I suggested. "You two could have a huge meal before starting your diet." And I laughed.

"You have no compassion, Robbie," Mike declared. "No compassion at all. Poor Cookie. He admires you above any other woman in the world. And you run off and marry an American. How could you!?!"

"Don't worry," I said casually. "I haven't been formally introduced to him yet. But I could be at any minute."

"Well, we better get over there right away and arrest him," Mike suggested to Jeff. "We can't allow him to steal our girl."

We all laughed, and then the men again became serious, continuing to discuss how they could help Angela in this challenging time. She needed to know that being physically abused is unacceptable, even if she was under the impression that she had caused all the problems in the relationship. No, that thinking was totally wrong. I felt outraged that it had happened to a family member. How dare that guy hurt my sister, I raged. I felt such fury within me that my muscles twitched and popped with energetic movement. I could not stay still. I needed something to take my mind off this situation. So, I went into my bedroom to do my research on Mr Eli Evans, who was from the USA.

CHAPTER TWO

"Ouch, Benny, you rascal," I scolded the little orange cat as he jumped through my bedroom window and onto my knee. He had wandered over the fence from his home with Miriam and the rabbi. "That hurt!" I complained. His nails are long and sharp. For some moments, I rubbed my legs while Benny smooched up to me so I would quickly forgive him. I always do, and he knows it, even though he sheds his fur everywhere in my bedroom. Also, he is aware that I have a packet of cat treats in my drawer. So, he is ready at any moment to lavish all his loving on me for his reward. He is very active, and for some time, he walked around, doing an intricate investigation of the entire room. I knew that this was the wrong time to open the digital tablet because Benny would walk all over it, causing me to lose what I had opened. Then he would plop himself down on top of it, relax and go to sleep. I would have to bribe him with treats to get him to move. Opening the drawer, I took out the packet and shook it a few times. Suddenly, the little scallywag was right there. Eagerly, he waited for his prize. So, I put a few treats on the sunniest part of the bed and hoped that he would settle down there, and he did. I felt my whole body relax, and I heaved a big sigh of relief. I was tempted to tell him that he was a good boy but thought better of it. I feared that if I were to speak to him, he might get the idea that I was inviting him to sit in my lap again. So, I quickly took the opportunity to unlock my digital tablet and prepare to do some work.

Opening the search engine, I typed the name, Eli Evans. And there he was. Yes, just the same as it was with the television evangelist Abby Jacobson. Many different sites talked extensively about him. First, I learned that he lived in Dallas, Texas. In my research, I have noticed that many famous Christian ministers who seem to be in top leadership roles, live in Texas. Mind you, Texas covers a large area (2.5 times that of New Zealand!) and has over a thousand cities, towns and villages. Not all of these people live in the largest cities. Yet they appear to know each other well, even though they are spread out, many living in much smaller towns. It is fascinating to look at the dynamics and see where they fit in.

Eli Evans was born in Saint Paul, Minnesota, in 1955. His parents were both teachers, enriched with backgrounds in mathematics and economics. Therefore, the family lived quite comfortably. Their beliefs were more of a philanthropic nature rather than based on religion. So, Eli never went to church or had any religious instruction when he was a child. But at high school, there was a very active Christian club. This was the early 1970s. Across the nation, many new churches were being birthed. There appeared to be a deep desire to know God in a fresh new way. Momentarily, I wondered whether this could have been a follow-on from the Jesus Movement of the 1960s.

To discover the correct information, I read historical accounts of this era and biographical stories of those who had risen to prominence in this emergence of a different Christian culture. A fresh emphasis was placed on the need for a personal commitment to God and an ongoing relationship with Him. It was no longer good enough to attend church once a week just for the sake of tradition. A particular significance was placed on evangelism; it was every believer's responsibility to tell people the good news.

While at college, Eli and his best friend Michael Cotes had been invited to an evangelistic crusade featuring a popular Christian worship band. It was there, Eli had said in an interview, that he and his friend had given their lives to Jesus Christ.

In their teenage years, the two young men worked well as a team and were highly respected in the community. One of their most successful ventures was their little business called *Up And Running*. After school and on weekends, they would feed the poor and elderly, organising groceries and doing extra work where needed. Eli always said that this was one of the most rewarding times of his life. Yet, in later years, they both took different career paths. Michael became a family doctor and moved to Gary, Indiana, while Eli studied law and became a successful attorney.

One day, a young woman walked into his office. Her name was Shea, and she was very beautiful. Eli was awestruck and found it difficult to turn his gaze away so he could attend to business. Shea lived in Dallas, Texas. She had travelled nearly 1,700 kilometres across the country to help her aunt. The elderly woman had been scammed out of most of her life savings by a scoundrel she had met on a cruise around the Greek Islands. It was a very distressing story.

The following month, Eli decided to travel to Dallas to visit Shea, and as he says, the rest is history. He packed up, moved across the country, and he and Shea got married. At first, Eli wasn't sure where his life was headed in this new place. There were many paths he could take. But then he was head-hunted by a large firm in the oil business. He worked there for almost ten years. It was a good life, and he and Shea were happy. Yet there was a deep discontentment in his soul, and he felt that he was not achieving all that he could in his life. So, he began to ask God about it in prayer. He felt impressed that he was to leave the firm and launch his own consulting company to assist people in the business and non-profit sectors. His vision was to help others reach their goals and provide a supportive team to those struggling in their goals to become successful in business.

Today, he is a very sought-after speaker and has written many books. He credits his success to his relationship with his God, who directs his path. He believes that God created him with gifts that he can use in a natural way to enrich the lives of others. He also refers back to when he and Michael worked together to give something unique to the community. Yes, I found him to be such a fascinating character, someone I might investigate more.

I closed down the computer and headed out to go next door. The sun streaked across my wheelchair, giving its heat to the armrests, and I sensed that if I stayed outside too long, it would burn my skin. Miriam was waiting at the door to greet me as I came up the ramp. We went into the kitchen, where Eli was sitting at the table, drinking his coffee. He pushed a chair out of the way so I could sit beside him.

"Hello," he said. "I'm glad you came back. Samuel has been telling me all about you. He says you are very clever. I hope we can get to know each other while I'm here."

I laughed. Yes, I was glad to have the opportunity to chat with him too.

"You are pretty interesting yourself," I replied.

"See, I told you that Robbie would quickly find out about you," exclaimed the rabbi. He stood at the kitchen door, laughing to himself. "And she met you only this morning."

Eli sat forward, his arms crossed, and with a cheeky smile, he dared me to tell him more. His eyes were warm and inviting, and his playful spirit endeared him to me. There was a great deal about him that I liked.

"So, tell me what you know," he enquired.

"You have a friend called Michael, who is a doctor," I told him. "The pair of you had a business called *Up and Running* when you were young."

Rabbi Mirsky looked over at Eli in surprise. He obviously didn't know about this part of his friend's story. Eli smiled and nodded. He seemed amused that I had chosen that particular information to reveal.

"I think you and I are going to become very good friends," he said.

"In some of the videos that you've done, you are in a huge library. Where is that?" I wanted to know.

"That is my office. Yes, I do have an extensive library," Eli asserted. "Some of those books are to help me write my research work. But others are for my pleasure. You like to read, don't you? And you research very well."

"I do okay, but I only research the things that interest me." I felt a little embarrassed to have so many people compliment me on my work. So, I tried to shift the conversation away from being about me. "Now, getting back to this library of yours," I said. "Have you read most of the books, or are they just gathering dust?"

But Eli was having none of it, and he switched the subject back to being about me and my life.

"Don't put yourself down, Robbie. You do well with what you do," he encouraged. "I think you can go on and do many great things that could influence the world for the good of others." Eli spoke these words with such veracity and expression that I felt energised. These words were like a healing balm to my soul, providing me with an overwhelming desire to stand up straight and dance. It was a strange feeling that stayed with me for quite some time.

Just then, Miriam began putting food on the table. There were scones, large portions of different kinds of cake and fresh fruits for those of us who wanted to eat healthy. Eli picked up a piece of lemon cake and took a bite. I could tell that he wasn't interested in eating healthy.

"So, tell me more about some of your books. You have so many," I pumped him. "What type of subjects interest you? Are you a sci-fi man, a romantic, or do you just read this New-Age Christian stuff that's very popular at the moment?"

"I enjoy reading about historical world events and people," he informed me. "And I am particularly interested in what will happen in the future."

"Oh, okay. Interesting." And I laughed. "You know, with a library that large, you could open it up to the public, charge and make heaps of money. Have you ever considered that?"

Eli rolled his eyes as the rabbi and Miriam chuckled.

"You sound like Shea," he moaned. "She says the same thing every time I bring a new book home. A couple of weeks ago, I came home with three books, and she suggested that we have a book sale and that I should donate all the profits to her favourite charity."

"Yes, but… Imagine all that dust!" I protested. "If that were Mom, just looking at those dusty shelves would send her into panic mode. The cleaning products would come out, and she would scrub them until you could see yourself in the wood like a mirror."

"I wouldn't like that job either," said Miriam. "I'm not a cleaning fanatic. With a job like that, I would have to hire a cleaning company."

"Very wise," I concurred. "Men have no idea how much work they make for the women of this world."

"Ohh, really?" Eli immediately sprang into a defensive mode. "And what about all the things we do for you? They don't count, I suppose."

"Of course, they do," I assured him. "We absolutely appreciate everything you do for us. But you just don't see dust. And that's a huge problem for us."

"I see," He laughed heartily, and his incorrigible smile told me that he didn't believe a word of what I was saying, but he would not pursue the subject right now. For some moments, he was silent, seemingly deep in thought about something specific. Then he jumped into gear again. Obviously, he had worked it all out in his mind and was ready to discuss his thoughts. "I'd like to work with you on a project," he said to me. "What do you think? Would you be interested in something like that?"

I nodded. This did sound interesting. *What sort of project could he be talking about?* I wondered. Patiently, I waited for his next piece of information. An interesting thing about Eli is his very expressive way of using his hands, even when silently thinking. It is fascinating to watch. Every little action is pronounced. His eyes flash with delight at the wonderment of things swirling around in his brain.

"I am working on an idea for a book," he said. "Samuel says that you have read the Bible quite extensively," he added. "Have you read the story of Joseph in Genesis 37-50?"

I nodded. Yes, I had read that story.

"Well, you will remember that it is about the guy who was sold to Midianite traders by his brothers, taken to Egypt and then sold to Potiphar to be his slave. A totally fascinating account."

"Yes, that happened because he had a big mouth," I laughed. "In my opinion, Joseph was the author of many of his own troubles. Perhaps if he hadn't boasted about being the top guy in his dreams, he might not have ignited the anger of his brothers. The story reminds me of someone else that you know personally. He lives in the Caribbean and is president of Morgandy. Now, he is a weird one."

"Oh, you mean President Boyd. Yes, he does seem to rub people the wrong way. No one is perfect, Robbie," he replied. "But God uses imperfect people to bring about good outcomes that He has planned for this mixed-up world. You can see that all through the Bible."

Suddenly, a comical idea popped into my head. *Yes*, I thought, *They would enjoy that.*

"Wouldn't it have been fun if there had been Twitter and paparazzi in Joseph's time?" I suggested. "I can see it now. The story might go like this. Firstly, there would be the high-profile missing person investigation. Who killed Joseph, and where is the body? Nevertheless, no leads ever surface. Seven years later, he would be declared legally dead, and the case closed. Yet there would be one detective who could not let it go. So, he formed a Cold Case Unit and searched high and low for Joseph. One day, five years later, he gets a call from an FBI agent, who tells him that Joseph's DNA and fingerprints have come up as a positive match for a prisoner in an Egyptian prison. Apparently, he was doing a long stretch for rape. The old detective took the first donkey to Egypt, but when he got to the prison, Joseph had already been released, pardoned by the Pharaoh. An informant relayed the story to the old detective. He said that the Pharaoh had a very vivid dream. However, later, he couldn't remember what it had been about. So, he called his spiritual advisers to tell him. They had no idea. Then Pharaoh's wine taster told him that he had been in jail with a guy that could interpret dreams. This greatly interested the Pharaoh and ordered Joseph to be brought to him. Yes, Joseph was not only able to tell the Pharaoh what the dream was, but what it meant for the future of Egypt. The Pharaoh was impressed and saw Joseph's great potential in business. So, he made him Prime Minister of Egypt.

"Now, I know that it doesn't say this in the Bible, but I believe that in his first tweet, Joseph would have let the world know that he had sacked all the spiritualist advisers because they couldn't get the job done. His next tweet would have advised the world that all borders were closed to family members with murderous intent. Finally, he would have declared that he was doing such a fantastic job as Prime Minister and that there was no one else who could have done it better."

By now, everyone was laughing.

"Well, that's another mystery solved," said the rabbi through all the chuckles. Miriam was laughing so much that she couldn't speak. Eli leaned forward and put his elbows on the table. I could tell he had enjoyed my rendition of the story of Joseph. His eyes eagerly sought my attention.

"That is the most interesting version of Joseph's story I have ever heard," he declared. "You have an extraordinary imagination. Perhaps we should pursue this conversation further. Tell me what else you know."

"You'll need to be more specific," I laughed. "I can't read your mind. So, what do you want to know?" The atmosphere was light and inviting, a good-humoured interaction.

"Eli wants to know all about that disastrous camp you go to every year," said the rabbi. Then he turned to his friend. "The strangest people run it."

"Oh well, yes. You are talking about Camp Run-A-Muck," I informed them. "Pete and I have been there twice now. But we are going to Elevate Christian Camp this year.

"Who is Pete," Eli enquired. "Someone special?"

"Boyfriend." Miriam nodded, indicating that she had full knowledge of all the details.

"Oh, serious, eh?" And he smiled to himself. "Are you planning to get married in the future?"

"My policemen friends want me to marry Cookie from the Hungry Horse Restaurant," I informed them. "They say that he is in love with me, and if I marry him, he will stay happy, and this will ensure that those in the Police Department always get a good meal at lunchtime."

"Poor Pete. So, where does this leave him?"

"Oh, not a problem." My reply was lighthearted and playful. "I'll just marry them both."

"Well, I hope I'm invited to that wedding," Eli laughed.

"Me too," the rabbi agreed. "I will keep that date free so that I can attend."

"I will need a new dress," said Miriam. "Yes, I certainly will." She smiled to herself as she replenished her cup of tea.

"So, tell me all about Camp Run-A-Muck," Eli encouraged me. "It sounds like a fun experience." He relaxed back into the comfort of the chair, and it creaked under his weight. All the while, he looked expectantly at me for all the relevant details. Yes, I could tell that he had a great curiosity and desire to learn about all things new and interesting. Well, I could tell him a lot. Oh yes, and I certainly would.

"A fun experience? Not if you are four days in and you haven't had a decent meal yet," I said. "It was more like diabolical!" A shiver went through me as I recalled my times in the dining room and the food set before me. "Cold baked beans and toast like cardboard."

Eli screwed up his nose, and Miriam frowned.

"Didn't they employ a decent cook?" asked Eli. "I assume that you had paid good money to stay there."

"Oh yes, there was a cook, so to speak," I replied. "Mrs Wrightson was her name. I don't know what she actually did, but whatever it was, she didn't do it in the kitchen. One night, my friend and I went to see if we could find something to eat. It had been a difficult day. So, I lay down to have a snooze. It was late in the afternoon, and I slept through dinner, such as it was. Well, we looked everywhere in that kitchen, and we were shocked. The cupboards and fridge were empty."

"So, what did you do?" Eli wanted to know.

"We drove into town to get burgers and chips. Mrs Wrightson appeared as we were getting into the car." I laughed as I remembered that incident, and everyone leaned in, anxious to know more. "She thought that I was homesick and going home. My friend told her that we were going to the pub. The look on her face was priceless. Indeed, she thought that I was intellectually disabled and couldn't understand anything that was going on around me."

Everyone laughed, and the rabbi shook his head in wonder.

"How strange," Miriam commented. "Did she ever talk to you?"

"No." This memory wasn't so funny. "But she talked to Pete about me," I informed her. "And she made him very angry."

"What did she say that was so bad?" Eli enquired.

"She praised him for taking the time to be a friend to me, a poor little intellectually handicapped child who probably didn't understand a word he was saying,"

"Wow." Eli was clearly affected by this. He looked as though he might break down and cry. "Wow," he repeated. "I'm speechless!" And he stared thoughtfully out the window, then with wonder at me, not uttering another word for some time.

"Well, we know different," Miriam declared. "She was just a silly woman who didn't take the time to see the truth about you. But you triumphed in the end, isn't that right?" And she nodded as she answered her own question. "Yes, when you went to camp last year, the food was much better," she added, signalling that this made her happy. I also indicated my agreement.

"Yes, it was great when Dad turned up, bringing Cookie and his restaurant staff. They even brought the food with them." I laughed as my mind wandered back to thoughts concerning the camp of the previous year. Suddenly, I saw Eli's face light up. His eyes sparkled as he spied a fresh array of Miriam's cupcakes that she had just taken out of the oven. He chose one and took a bite.

"I like Miriam's cooking best," he declared. "Even though I have never tried Cookie's food, she is my top chef."

"Oh yes," the rabbi agreed. "I never need to go to Cookie's restaurant."

Miriam laughed, perhaps feeling a little embarrassed, receiving so much praise. But I was pleased that the men happily acknowledged her gifts, admiring and honouring her this way. I could see that it meant a great deal to Miriam as well.

"Yes, Miriam's cooking is far superior to Cookie's," I concurred. "It's the woman's touch that does it every time." The guys nodded their agreement and smiled with contentment. Then I turned to Eli. "So, what brings you to New Zealand?" I wanted to know.

"It was the memory of Miriam's cooking," Eli replied. "And knowing she would have some delightful friends like yourself to visit." Then he added. "I couldn't help myself. I had to come. And here I am." I stared at him disbelieving. *Oh, yeah*, I thought. He was now sporting that roguish fun look that unites friends, so that they enjoy being together. Yes, I did like Eli.

CHAPTER THREE

As I was leaving the rabbi's house, by chance, I glanced across the road to my left. No, I did not like what I saw. A new car was parked not far from where I lived, and an individual was sitting in the driver's seat. He was looking furtively at our house. Then he would pop down out of sight so that he couldn't be easily spotted. I hadn't seen him before and didn't recognise the car. It looked somewhat suspicious to me. Miriam was with me, and I told her that we must go back inside and that I needed to talk to the rabbi. The two men were surprised to see me again but pushed a chair aside so that I could sit at the table.

"Robbie wants to talk to you, Samuel," said Miriam. And then she sat down herself. All three looked at me with anticipation.

"Could you please ring my dad and tell him that a suspicious guy is in a car watching our house? It could be nothing, but my guess is that it is that wicked boyfriend of my sister. He is probably waiting for her to leave the house so that he can abduct her."

"Oh yes, I will do that straight away." He took his phone out of his pocket and rang Dad's number. Meanwhile, Eli went outside to look around. A few moments later, he appeared again.

"Yes," he said. "When the guy saw me looking his way, he ducked out of sight. He must think we are all blind and can't see him sitting there. Oh, and across the road, another neighbour was also keeping an eye on him. I could see her peeking through the lace curtains, taking in every piece of information she could gather." And he laughed. "She let go of the curtain and stepped back when I looked closer in her direction. I don't think she wanted me to see her either."

"That's Tania," Miriam informed him. "Was she holding a wine glass? She was probably drunk. Come to think of it, she is always drunk whenever I see her. No, she won't remember anything by tomorrow."

I smiled to myself but didn't comment. Miriam had said it all quite perfectly. Tania and Brian, her husband, were no longer together since he discovered his wife's affair with Larry, the neighbour a few doors away. What's more, he had taken custody of Jojo, the dog.

Of course, I shouldn't be gossiping about things like this. But when I remember back to the day of the big tennis match between Larry the Larrikin and Chewing Gum Charlie, I have trouble keeping a straight face. Brian had boldly walked into the tennis courts to confront Larry about fooling around with his wife. There were no words spoken between the two men. A deathly hush fell in the stadium as they stared at each other and considered what each one would do next. Although it seemed a long time, they stood eye to eye for perhaps only a few seconds before Brian took his chance. He threw a heavy right hook to the jaw, and Larry went down like a pack of cards. Our town is somewhat small and over half the village folk had turned out to see the tennis match. Well, the crowd was abuzz with whispering and intermittent giggling. This was a show that none of us would have missed. Ultimately, the tennis match couldn't be completed because Larry was laid out in all his glory on the hard court, eyes closed and unresponsive. For several minutes, none of us dared move. But I strained forward to see Larry's face. Yes, he definitely was out cold, I concluded. Meanwhile, Chewing Gum Charlie was ecstatic because it meant that he could claim the victory. I disagree. Brian was the winner that day. He had been cool, calm and collected and had taken his revenge on his rival without uttering a word. Afterwards, he walked over to the policemen, turned around, put his hands behind his back, and waited to be cuffed.

When Brian left the family home, Tania's life appeared to crumble. I understand that she and Larry are no longer an item, and in her loneliness, she has succumbed to drinking any alcohol that she can get her hands on. It is tragic. Sometimes, when she has had too many drinks, she comes out and screams abuse at the neighbours. We don't know which neighbours she is targeting. She is so wasted that her words don't form properly and cannot be easily understood. Almost everyone in the street has something to say about her, but no one wants to actually get involved in helping her; what a shame. She desperately needs help.

Before long, we heard Dad arrive and park in our driveway next door. Soon afterwards, Mike and Jeff came, parking the police car strategically in front of our house. The two policemen walked over to the suspect's car and talked at length with the guy, taking all his details and instructing him to leave the area. They did not arrest him at this time. I assume they let him go because they needed Angela to make a formal complaint. He sped away in his car, and I thought, *Well, I hope this will be the last we see of him.* Again, the neighbourhood fell silent, and I felt safe.

That afternoon, I decided to go to the mall. It was a beautiful day, and I was eager to see who was out and about. I felt very contented as I admired the gardens and all the foliage from the trees and bushes. It was the fragrance of life. Even the fresh air had its own special aroma. Looking at life realistically, I find it difficult to believe that this world and humans were created from a huge explosion of space dust. I look at the intricate way that the earth and its inhabitants are made and function. It is amazing. Christians and Jewish people who follow the Hebrew faith say that there is a great Designer who created all this, yet he can't be seen as a physical entity. This is somewhat difficult for me to comprehend. My little mind can only absorb so much, and the reality of a Creator who is everywhere but can't be seen is a bit much for me at the moment. I will work it out eventually. There is no doubt about that. So, the jury is still out. Meanwhile, I will enjoy all the wonderful sights in this world and continue to live a happy life.

Entering the Mall, I headed towards my favourite clothes shop. Yes, I wanted to check out their latest stock. I was about to go inside when a man stepped out of the shadows and stood in front of me. Suddenly, I felt afraid. This man had a bad vibe, and I sensed that he might hurt me if he had the chance to do so.

"Tell your sister that I want to see her," he blurted out. "And we don't need the cops involved. Understand? No cops. Someone could get hurt."

I didn't say a word, and out of the corner of my eye, I could see Shirley, the shop assistant looking my way. She was now ringing someone on her cell phone. So, I relaxed. Yes, she had the situation covered now. Soon, Billy, the guard, appeared and asked me if I was having a good day. I nodded, and he suggested that we should go and have a coffee. The guy, who was, of course, Angela's boyfriend, had retreated again into the shadows. No problem. I knew where he was. So, when Mike and Jeff turned up, I was able to point them in the right direction.

I cut short my shopping expedition that day and headed home. Nearing the house, I changed my mind and decided to visit Miriam instead. She welcomed me into her kitchen and sat with me at the table. Soon the rabbi and Eli joined us, and the fun and the banter of friendship began again. Seeing the relaxed and smiling faces and knowing I was safe, felt good. Yes, I did feel somewhat shaken by the events at the mall. I realised that Angela's boyfriend was very dangerous, and I was fortunate to get out of that situation as well as I did. Just then, the rabbi's cell phone rang. From what I could hear, it was my dad.

"Yes, she is here," the rabbi said. Then he listened as Dad updated him on the situation in our household and the wicked boyfriend. "We will look after her. Don't worry. She can stay with us until you get this sorted," he assured Dad. They spoke for a couple of minutes longer and then said their goodbyes.

"I hear that you have had an adventure this afternoon, Robbie," the rabbi commented.

"That crazy guy, who beat up Angela, threatened me," I informed them. "He was scarier than the guy who was sent to kill me a few months ago."

"What?!" Eli was shocked." Who was sent to kill you?" he wanted to know.

"Oh, that was Timothy Sweeney. He couldn't kill a fly," I told him. "When I discovered he was following me, I cornered him and ran over his foot several times." The memory of it tickled my funny bone, and I chuckled as I relayed the story to him. "My wheelchair is very heavy and would have seriously injured his foot. Mike, my policeman friend, tells me that he is still in custody, in prison somewhere in another part of the country. And he is wearing the latest style in plaster cast and moon boot."

My three friends were amused. Then the rabbi became more serious.

"Would you like to come to stay with us for a few days?" he asked me. "You and Eli could get better acquainted."

I was taken by surprise, but yes, I was very interested to find out more about Eli. And I didn't know how long he would be here in New Zealand.

"Do you have the room here?" I wanted to know. "You already have a guest. It could be too much for you."

"Oh, Eli's not a guest," Miriam stated. "He's family. And there is plenty of room here. We would love to have you stay."

Everything being settled, I would go home later to pack my gear.

"Are you working on anything special while you are here?" I asked Eli. I knew that he would be, but I wanted him to tell me about it.

"Oh yes," he assured me. "I have a very important assignment right here in New Zealand."

"Tell me more," was my reply.

"I want to know all about you," he said. "You can teach me so much about your life as a disabled woman."

"Wow!! That will be a quick study," I laughed. "There is not much to know about me. Now, you are another matter. There is a whole lot that I don't know about you yet."

"You seem to handle your disability well. Tell me about that."

"I have had Cerebral Palsy all my life, so I don't really know life without it," I informed him. "Although I did walk and dance for a short time when I visited that special garden."

"What garden was that?" Eli's eyes lit up. He was very interested now.

"I had an accident, and I was unconscious for a while. It was then that I went to the garden and met the man who knew everyone I knew. He took me on a tour of his garden. It was beautiful. Then he took me to a concert and talked to me about Charlie, the opera singer. Charlie had cancer, but he didn't know it yet."

"So, was Charlie a family friend?" Eli wanted to know.

"No. He only came to stay when I was unconscious." I laughed to myself as I recalled how Charlie and I had met. "He was sitting in my room when I woke up. I couldn't believe my eyes."

"I can imagine," he said. His eyes danced with joy as he sought to know more of my story. "And so, in the garden, were you able to walk around freely and use your hands?"

"Oh yes. It was easy. I was able to touch the flowers without breaking them and the path that I walked along was like crystal. The colours were so bright and made me happy. It was so beautiful there. I wanted to stay, but the man whose garden it was, told me that I had to come back. He said that I must come back and create a future for myself. He told me to move mountains."

"Did you know you would still be disabled when you came back?" he asked.

"Yes. I knew by the way he was talking to me."

"What else did he say?

"He told me to walk in his footsteps because he can help me to become the person that I was born to be. He said that even with my disability, if I allow him, he is able to make me strong so that I can do great things."

Eli nodded and smiled to himself, pausing for just a few moments to absorb and process what I had said. He had his own thoughts and opinions but wasn't ready yet to bring them forward. If there is one thing I admire about Eli, he listens well; not pushy with his own agenda of how things should go; and he makes me smile with his excitable childlike nature. He expresses such joy in his discoveries, and he brings everyone around him in to share all his 'aha' moments.

"So, who is this man that you met? Do you know?" His question was genuine, and he was trying to encourage me to think things through.

"He's the King," I replied assuredly. "A special king. And a very memorable person to have met."

"A king of where? If he was a king, he must have had a kingdom, a place to reside. Do you know where this garden was situated?"

"Okay, well, I hadn't thought that far," I informed him. "But I don't think it was Heaven or where the Christians go. I've met some of Mom's Christian friends. Crazy, crazy, crazy. No, this was a real place with sensible people living in it. Oh no. No weirdos lived there."

Everyone laughed, and Miriam made more coffee and refreshed the dishes with more cake. This amused me, as I visualised just how big Eli would be when he returned to the USA. If Shea was anything like my mom, who tries to keep Dad's diet on a tight rein, I imagine she might not be pleased.

"Are you disappointed that you have your disability back?" he wanted to know. The rabbi nodded his agreement. It was obvious that he, too, was interested in learning what my answer might be.

"Yes, I was unhappy about it at first," I confessed. "It was tough to come back to a life of disability, especially when I had experienced having the ability to do all the things I have never done before. So, I told God that if I couldn't have that, I'll have the next best thing."

"And what would that be?" the rabbi wanted to know.

"I've decided I'm going to be a billionaire," I joked. "Yes, Sir. That's my plan. I've read that you know a few people in that category. President Boyd, maybe?" And I looked at Eli with my most mischievous grin. "Perhaps you could ask him if he would like to adopt me." Then I sat back and waited to hear the remarks. I expected to get some good reactions. The rabbi sat back in quiet repose.

"President Boyd's financial portfolio is well within her desired dreams," he commented. I could see that he was holding back his laughter.

"True, true." Eli nodded in agreement. "I will mention it when I see him, later this month. Can you wait that long?"

"I hope you don't forget us when you are living in your mansion," said Miriam. I could tell that she was enjoying our lively banter. But I noticed that Eli was in quiet contemplation. *What could he be thinking about?* I wondered. He kept looking at me and turning away. At this time, Miriam and I were discussing other things of the day, trivial things that women find interesting. Yes, it did appear that I was on Eli's mind. Perhaps he was trying to find a way to steer the discussion back in the direction of other things that he wanted me to tell him about my visit to the garden. But I was way ahead of him. Yes, I could tell that he was after more information about these things and perhaps my own personal journey in studying the Bible. And he had enjoyed my version of the Bible story of Joseph and the tweets. Now, he wanted to know if the stories that I had read had resonated with me in a positive way and changed my opinion about God, Jesus and the Christian Faith. Well, I was going to make him wait. At that moment, I was having too much fun making them all laugh.

Just then, someone knocked on the front door. The rabbi went to answer it, and Miriam filled the electric jug with water, ready to make a fresh pot of tea. The rabbi appeared, followed by Dad. They both sat down at the table, and Miriam gave Dad a cup of tea.

"Your mother sent me with a bag of things you may need tonight," he said to me. "Let us know if anything is missing."

I nodded.

"Is Angela okay?"

"Yes, that no-good boyfriend is in custody right now," he revealed. "We are very thankful that you noticed him when you did. He was planning to kidnap her and take her back to Wellington." He looked concerned and somewhat stressed, unlike the usual happy-go-lucky dad, who was always joking and laughing. It was a sad sight, and I suddenly wanted to cry.

"We will keep a good eye on your house," the rabbi assured Dad, and he seemed to relax a little. I think he needed that reassurance, the knowledge that others were standing with him during this difficult time.

"Thank you. Your help is so appreciated." Dad looked longingly at the plate of Miriam's cupcakes for a few moments, then reached over to pick his favourite. This was more like the dad of old. I felt better and happier.

"Robbie has been sharing her plans for the future with us." The rabbi's words were peppered with intermittent chimes of laughter.

"Oh really!" Dad exclaimed. "She hasn't mentioned anything to us. Does it include great amounts of money? We need someone to look after us in our old age." And then he picked up another of Miriam's delicious cupcakes. Mom would not be pleased if she were to witness this. She had recently put him on a strict diet, and cakes were off the menu.

"Oh yes," the rabbi assured him. "She is going to be a billionaire."

"Fantastic!" Dad looked at me with renewed interest. "I will be able to retire early." He seemed delighted as he took another bite. However, I could see that he was waiting for more information. "Do you have a ballpark date when this might happen?" he wanted to know. "When should I put the garage on the market?"

"She is considering looking into the possibility of being adopted by Eli's friend, President Boyd from Morgandy," said Miriam. "We want visitors' rights."

By now, everyone was tittering and giggling. I just sat there, stoically waiting for the right moment to confirm or deny the whole thing. Dad turned to Eli and smiled.

"Great," he responded. "I can leave everything in your capable hands then, since President Boyd is your friend. Just let us know when we can move into the mansion."

Later that night, I settled into the second spare bedroom, and Miriam came in to see if there was anything that I needed. Her mothering instincts are always active, no matter who the person might be. She truly has a compassionate heart, sensitive and generous. So, nothing is too much for her to do. I can see why those who know her love her so much.

"Samuel and I are taking Eli to Hamilton tomorrow," she said. "Would you like to come with us?"

Hamilton. My favourite city. Yes, I was all in for that. She said that we might have time to visit my friend April while we were there. Wow! That would be so cool, I thought. Miriam will enjoy our time with April. She would feel at home there, doing all the motherly things that make her happy.

It was only 8pm. The others in the household seemed to be retiring for the night; therefore, it seemed appropriate that I also should go to bed. I settled into the warm and comfy bed sheets, but I wasn't tired yet. So, I decided to open my digital tablet and check out who was on social media and what they were moaning about today. I am always amazed at how people get so upset at such trivial things. Many arguments eventuate because they disagree on personal issues of race, religion and politics. Or it can be any other subject that catches their interest at the time. Making noise and being noticed are all important to people on social media today. Oh yes. The usual suspects were very vocal tonight. I don't often get involved. Yet I like to know what is being said. Sometimes, I have difficulty keeping my mouth shut, especially if I think the truth is not being told. But it is not worth the trouble. All I want is a quiet, happy life. So, I just post comical pictures that amuse my friends, and animal stories that tug on the hearts of pet lovers.

Eli was in the bedroom next to mine. I could hear him as he prayed. I wasn't listening intentionally, but our rooms were very close, and he was vocalising his prayers. They were intensely personal, showing the depth of his commitment to God, his family and friends. He also talked to God about the problematic issues in the wider world that he sees daily. He has personally witnessed many of these situations as he travels around the world. It seems to me that these things, and a belief that he has a God-given assignment, have triggered his desire to set up his business. Standing beside people in times of hardship, he is able to share with them particular ways of making their business more viable and an easier path to success.

Suddenly, I heard Eli mention my name. I listened as he prayed for me, asking God to bless me and help me in everything I try to do. He also asked God to help him to know how to help me. This was huge in my estimation. Yes, I did know that his greatest desire was that I would become a Christian. There was no denying it. But Eli was prepared to move beyond that to doing special things just to make me happy and more comfortable in every way. I liked that. Yes, he truly was a nice man and a wise one too. If he was staying awhile, we would definitely be spending more time discussing interesting topics.

For some time, I lay there, thinking about my life and all that had happened to me over the years. Perhaps things had been difficult during some stages of my life. Yet there was a great deal that I should be thankful for, I thought. Other people I know personally, endure far worse events and disabilities than I could even imagine. I shiver when I recall some of their stories. No, I would not be able to cope in many of those circumstances. Yet here I was with Miriam and the rabbi. Sheltered by these beautiful people, they had opened their home, gathering me into their protection, holding me close as a hen does with her chicks. Yes, I was indeed blessed.

CHAPTER FOUR

Friday morning, and everyone was up early; all the chatter was about our trip to Hamilton. The rabbi would take Miriam and me to visit April. Then he and Eli would go to the University, where they would participate in a very important debate about politics in the Middle East. Men, eh! They always seem to be involved in some scheme to save the world. And we ladies are not invited to take part. Oh well. I suppose that it keeps them out of trouble.

We were eating breakfast when Eli received a call on his mobile phone. His eyes lit up when he saw who was calling. It was Shea.

"Oh, how I miss this lady," he said tenderly. "My sweet honey girl. I wish she were with me here." Then speaking directly into the phone. "Hello, my love." His face clouded as Shea explained why she had called. Unfortunately, there was terrible news. A close friend and his family from Houston, Texas, had been in a horrific car smash, and two of the children were in critical condition. The worry on Eli's face told me that he wished that he was at home right now. Yes, it was difficult for him to be so far away and unable to help or support in person. For some minutes after ending the call, he sat in quiet contemplation. He seemed hard-pressed to process it all. Then he began to talk about the family. Miriam suggested they spend a few minutes bringing their distress about the family and the accident to God. So, they began to pray, asking God to heal each child. Their expressions of genuine concern and compassion were quite remarkable. They seemed to be encased in a single moment in time where all thoughts and prayers align to bring about the desired result. Watching them, I became pretty emotional. Yes, their heartfelt words had undoubtedly touched me deeply.

I had closed my eyes and unwittingly, I was right with them in their prayer time. It just seemed the right thing to do. But every now and again, I opened one eye to check that I wasn't missing anything important. Then I closed it again, I suppose as a mark of respect. It was, I think, the third time that I looked that I saw something that shocked me. Standing behind Eli, there was a very large man. He wore an unusual robe-like garment that was knee length, Roman sandals and headgear, which suggested that he was probably a soldier from the New Testament times. I had read three of the Gospels and understood that Roman rulers dominated Israel at this time. He looked over at me and smiled, acknowledging me, inviting me to look deeper into his world and why he was sent. In his left hand, he was holding a large spear. One end rested on the floor as one would do with a walking stick. It was like I was part of an old-time religious movie, yet only half the people in the room were dressed in character. So, I closed my eyes again, hoping to adjust my sight. Maybe my mind was not visualising correctly.

Madness. I had never seen this side of me before. Slowly, I opened my eyes once more and looked around. Yes, he was still there, and now there were others. They stood more in the background, very attentively watching as each person talked to God about a different aspect of the accident and the serious condition of the children. Every time the person asked for God to do something, a soldier would disappear, and another would take his place. That was interesting, I thought. As I continued to watch, mesmerised, there was a growing hunger within me to find out more. What would happen next? Then I saw something that I hadn't noticed before. Whenever anyone mentioned the name Jesus or Yeshua, the soldiers would instantly stand to attention. Now, I hadn't nodded off and wasn't having a daydream. No, I really was seeing these men. And as far as I know, I am not crazy, although others may not agree. I laughed to myself as I considered what people might say if I were to mention it.

So, there I was, witnessing something quite extraordinary. A few minutes later, the prayer time ended, and all the soldiers disappeared. I was both relieved and disappointed at the same time, if you can make sense of that. It was a relief to me that I was no longer having strange visions. Yet, I would have liked to know more about the visitors and the purpose of their presence. That being said, I decided not to say anything about it for the moment. I didn't want people to think that I had totally lost my mind.

As we continued eating our breakfast, Eli talked more about his friends. It was obvious that he was very close to the family. The children were nine and seven years old. Tyson, the older boy, loved to paint. His school teacher Mrs Smith was very proud of the artwork that he had done in her class. She believed that he had a gift, a natural flair for many things creative. She arranged for her students to try clay art. Most of the children made monsters or animals. She had related to the family that for a few moments, Tyson had studied her face and then he began to work with the clay. Within minutes he had made a realistic bust of her. Mrs Smith was amazed and suggested to his parents that they arrange for him to have formal art lessons. His brother Toby was the scoundrel in the family. He was often up to something mischievous, doing things which perhaps didn't quite turn out the way he wanted. Yet, he always made everyone smile. One day, he went to the market with his mother to get milk and bread. While in line, waiting to pay, he noticed an old lady who was standing in line at the checkout. She clearly didn't have enough money in her purse to pay for her food.

"Mama," he said in a very loud voice that echoed throughout the store, "we should help that poor lady because Jesus helps us when we are broke." From what I understand, Toby's mother gulped and looked around in embarrassment. She wished she was invisible for a moment, but quickly pulled herself together.

"Yes," she replied. "Let's do that." And she gave him a big hug. However, before she could do anything, several other people had given the lady the money for her food and even more. Nevertheless, to show her son that they must always follow through with their promise, she took his hand, walked over to the lady and gave her twenty dollars. Eli told us that both parents, James and Sharon, were so proud of Toby for his kindness that day, and they talked about it a lot. Now the two boys were fighting for their lives in hospital, and everyone was so concerned.

"They are going to be alright, you know," I informed them. The rabbi, Eli and Miriam looked over at me with renewed interest. Good news is always welcome, but I wasn't sure that they truly believed me. Perhaps not. Miriam rubbed my arm and searched my eyes sympathetically.

"The boys are in God's hands now," she said quietly. "Whatever He chooses will be fine. He knows best."

"No," I insisted. "The boys are going to live and be okay," A part of me was irritated that there was some doubt about what I was telling them. In truth, I had no idea how I knew this, but something within my soul assured me that there would be a good outcome and gave me the confidence to speak it out. Sensing my frustration, all three friends drew close, giving me their full attention.

"Tell me what you know," Eli enquired.

"You like to keep up with the latest gossip, eh?" I bantered with him.

"I call it staying informed," he responded. "You know something more than we do, and I would like you to share."

"Well, I don't know if they would like me to tell you."

"They?" Eli looked surprised. "Who are they?"

"The soldiers. You probably didn't see them because your eyes were closed when you prayed," I replied casually. I found talking about it easy. After all, it made perfect sense to me, as I was just relaying the facts of what I had seen.

"Oh, yes, that does make sense," Eli agreed. "So, soldiers were here while we prayed for the family. How many did you see?"

"Now, don't make fun of me," I warned. "I did see soldiers. There were about half a dozen, and they wore Roman uniforms."

"Wow, a feisty lady," Eli laughed as he turned to include Miriam and the rabbi. "I don't think I want to cross swords with her. I'd never survive." And he whistled and rolled his eyes.

"I wouldn't challenge her," said the rabbi. "If Robbie says that there were soldiers from Heaven here, then there were just that."

"Several soldiers were coming and going," I told them. "But the one who stood behind Eli stayed until the end of the prayers. He smiled at me, and I think he knew who I was."

"Aawww," Miriam uttered. "That is so special." Again, she gently rubbed my arm, letting me know she liked what I had said, even though she thought it might be a little far-fetched.

"Wow," Eli said again. "Yes, that is very special. And I do believe you." He was excited now. "Our prayer times are unique, because we are partnering with God and all of the heavenly angels to change a situation here on earth. So, everyone in heaven rejoices when we pray. Would you mind if I shared this with the family? It could encourage them in this difficult time. I will ring them."

I nodded, making sure that he knew that it was okay. Again, he took his mobile phone out of his pocket and rang a person from his contact list. It sounded like his friend was overseeing things for the family at the hospital. The boys' parents were also inpatients there; however, their injuries were not as bad. Eli and his friend spoke for about ten minutes or so. Ending the call, he looked more relaxed and happier. I sensed that something in the situation over there had shifted or perhaps changed for the better.

"Well, things are looking up," Eli informed us. "Toby is awake and talking like a book. He demanded to have chicken for his dinner. And Tyson has a broken leg and internal injuries, but his hands are okay. He will still be able to do his artwork."

Again, the three friends bowed their heads and thanked God for this great news. These were happy prayers, and everyone seemed infused with enthusiasm and expectation for the future. With the table cleared and dishes washed, we all prepared to go to Hamilton. I sat in the back seat of the car with Eli. He seemed very busy for the first fifteen minutes as he checked to see if he had any emails. Apparently, he had set his phone to alert him when there were any important news items he wanted to know about. I don't know how he did that. But it appeared to make him happy. At this point, I didn't ask any questions. I could tell he did a great deal of his personal communications on that phone. Then he went to his main social media account to see what people were saying there. He smiled to himself as he read the comments and posts on his page.

"We can say something about our trip on social media," said Eli. "Let's have some fun, eh?"

I laughed to myself. I had never been on a video like this before, and now, we were going to do a live broadcast. How fascinating! I was intrigued to see how it all worked. Presently, he opened up his phone, went to his social media page and turned on the camera. He pushed several buttons, and suddenly, I could see us both on the screen.

"Hello people," he opened his broadcast enthusiastically. "I'm in New Zealand, the jewel of the Pacific, thousands of miles from my home in Houston, Texas. My friends and I are driving to a city called Hamilton. Apparently, it is the fourth largest city in the country. We are going to a meeting at the University there." He looked quizzically out the windows, taking in the view. "Wow!" he exclaimed. "I'm overwhelmed! The countryside is so *green* here!" Then he turned his phone so that his online viewers could see the rolling hills and farmland. "I hope you can see this beautiful sight," he said. "I can't really tell. But I'm doing my best. And the scenery is certainly worth the time to show you." Quickly, he turned the phone back to where he could be seen. "So, my friends, Samuel and Miriam have introduced me to New Zealand's National Anthem," Eli continued. "This delightful couple are originally from Israel and came to live here about a year ago. Samuel tells me that there were many things that attracted them to this country. And the anthem was one of them. I can understand why. It is a beautiful prayer, and God is at the centre of it." Then he began to recite the verses clearly, so that his friends would understand. At that moment, I felt very proud to be a Kiwi and to have Eli as my new friend. He had taken the time to memorise the words of the anthem. I thought this was very commendable.

Yes, Eli is a remarkable man, and I have a great deal of respect for him. He is also knowledgeable about what the Bible teaches, steadfast in his Christian beliefs and ready to explain it all at any moment. Yet, he isn't overly pushy. Well, that is what I have found anyway. He treats me well as his friend.

The most amusing thing about Eli is his preoccupation with governmental issues of the little nation of Morgandy in the Caribbean, and this guy, President Boyd. But to be fair, Eli was one of the first Christian prophetic commentators in the world to predict that Jason Boyd would win the race for the presidency in 2011. Many did not believe him when he said that Mr Boyd was God's choice; some in the Christian community ridiculed him. Yet Eli stood fast on what he saw as God's plan for Morgandy, risking his reputation and livelihood. Against all odds, Mr Boyd became the 14th President, succeeding Mr Smyth, his great rival. So, it was quite natural for me to want to know more about this President. Of course, I didn't do a complete study at the time that I met Eli. No. Events in my life were moving so fast, that there wasn't enough time. This being the case, what I tell you now, I have learned over time, giving it a great deal of thought.

It is difficult not to notice, but President Boyd does have some unusual personality traits. This has caused him many serious problems in his presidency, and people have spoken publicly against him. Now, I have looked closely at this situation and have some thoughts on the matter. It occurs to me and is only my opinion, but I wonder if Mr Boyd may have a mild form of autism. This is where his mind works differently to his peers, and he is not so adept in some forms of communication. I have found that the wider community sometimes does have a problem with people of difference. There is the thought that if a person does not look like me, think like me, or act like me, then they are unacceptable. In the case of President Boyd, he does not tick all the boxes of what we expect as a president. Coupled with opponents that use every available weapon to destroy him and the press who enjoys magnifying every mistake he makes, then unless he is made of steel, refusing to be broken, he is, in fact, politically a dead man walking.

Eli sees President Boyd's problematic issues with those who seek to ruin him, somewhat differently. He believes they involve two warring factions in the heavenly realm, the battle between good and evil. There was once a time when I would have laughed at such a suggestion. But when I look at what is happening in the world today, I must admit that this could be true. How we live, think and treat each other is changing so fast that it is difficult to keep up. As the world has embraced advanced technology and we can communicate our thoughts more easily through social media, personal levels of respect and regard for others have dropped to an all-time low. Eli talks about this a lot. Turning my attention back to his broadcast, I listened intently.

"My friends around the world," he said. "We need to pray for disabled people everywhere, ASAP. The abortion laws are being changed in many nations and women will soon be able to choose to abort their baby up to the day of the birth. Then if the child has certain disabilities, the mother will have the choice to let them die. Can you imagine that?!" He then turned his phone, so that the camera would capture me.

"Here beside me is my new friend, Robbie. She is a great investigator and helps the Police solve crimes. Now, Robbie has Cerebral Palsy and lives what we would think to be an extremely difficult life. Yet she assures me that this is not the case. She lives a full and active life, has many friendships within the broader community and has a boyfriend whom she loves. The sad thing is, that for people like Robbie, the future is not secure. Under the new legislation, a child who has a severe disability that has been detected before birth, or found to be not quite right at birth, will be disposed of without penalty. Robbie tells me that she has a soft spot in her heart for people with Downs Syndrome. I know that they are very close to her heart and they love her too. She says that these precious people have the most beautiful hearts and deserve to live good lives. Yes, I believe there are serious problems, but Robbie says that with help, these things can be easily worked out.

"Having met Robbie and learning so much about her life as a disabled person," Eli continued. "I now appreciate my own life more and thank God for the wonderful way He has blessed me too. It appears that people like Robbie and her friends have skills and abilities that we can only dream of. Listen, people. What are we doing when we choose not to allow these babies to live? The Bible tells us that children are a gift from God. Yes, every good and perfect gift is from God. It also says that we are wonderfully and intricately made. I could go on and on about it. But truly, these things need to be said often and out loud. I know I have probably opened a can of worms as I discuss this particular issue. Yes, I will get some negative feedback. But I don't care. Let the knuckleheads try to shut me up. Now, I want you to tell me your stories. Tell me what you know! We are about to arrive at our destination in Hamilton. So, I will sign off now. Stay safe, my friends. Bye."

As we turned into the street where April lived, we were greeted by a line of police cars and a great deal of activity. One policeman was getting his dog out of the back of his van, while others were quickly walking towards the small village of elderly and disabled people. Suddenly, I was totally gripped with fear. Memories of the day that Joel died came flooding back. Surely, it couldn't be happening again. The rabbi stopped the car near the entrance to the little village and rolled down the window. Soon an officer came across to talk to us.

"We are dropping a couple at number twelve," the rabbi informed him. And he pointed in the direction of April's house. "We have a young lady here who has a wheelchair." He indicated that it was me, and the policeman looked my way, nodded and smiled.

"That'll be okay," he said. "We do have a problem, as you will have guessed. But it is at the house next door to the village."

I felt my whole body relax. April wasn't hurt. What a relief! But I was curious to know why the Police were there. As we neared our destination, I saw the car of April's friend Muriel parked in a space adjacent to a neighbour's house. Yes, she would know. Nothing escapes her notice. Miriam and I would be made aware of every detail before this visit was over.

CHAPTER FIVE

"Put your arms around my neck so that I can get you outta there quickly," said Eli. And he positioned himself so that he could easily take hold of me. It was somewhat awkward for poor Eli. He was a big man, and I was sitting in a little car. So, he had to work hard to manoeuvre his arms around my small frame. "It is just as well that you haven't been eating too many of Miriam's cakes," he added. "If you were any bigger, I could end up in hospital with a broken back." And he chuckled.

"Ohh, yeah, you think!!" I exclaimed. My body shook with laughter, making it more difficult for him to get a firm hold of me. "Who eats all Miriam's cakes?" I demanded to know. "It's not me, is it Miriam? No. It's the three musketeers, you, the rabbi and my dad. I will never be fat because you three eat all the cakes before I get the chance to have my share."

He was finally able to lift me out of my seat and put me in the manual wheelchair. I always need to use this when I go anywhere by car. The electric chair is big and heavy, so it can't be put in a regular car boot. I suppose we could have come in the van, which has a wheelchair hoist. We usually do, when going on long trips. It enables me to be independent, and others don't need to push me around in public continually. Anyway, I was enjoying it here beside Eli and watching him do his live video on social media.

Muriel suddenly appeared as we parked in front of April's house. She stood by expectantly as Eli settled me into the wheelchair.

"You've come at a very exciting time, Robbie," she remarked. "Did you glean any important information as you were driving in?" Then speaking directly to Eli. "We rely on Robbie to update us on what she knows, as she is special friends with the constabulary."

"No, not yet," I replied. "We want to know what you know."

Apparently, April had been sitting at the window all morning as she didn't want to miss a minute of what was happening next door. Excitedly, she had called Muriel on the phone. It's always great to share the latest news with a friend. So, Muriel came right over so that she could share in the fun. Since then, the two best friends had been watching all the comings and goings of the police personnel as they sought to arrest their suspects.

We all went inside, and Eli parked me next to April. Then Eli, Miriam and the rabbi settled themselves in comfortable chairs nearby. When introductions were over, April began her interrogations to find out more about my friends. I knew they wouldn't be able to leave until she learned everything there was to know about them. But that is the way she is. Where others would perhaps wait to be told what visitors wanted them to know, April jumps right in, requiring very detailed explanations about everything concerning their lives.

"Wow! What a great accent," she said to Eli. "Where in the USA are you from? And are you married? Tell us all about your life. We want to know everything." Her curiosity was undeniable, much like his. And her stare was all-encompassing.

"I live in Houston, Texas. But my hometown is Saint Paul, Minnesota. And yes, I am married to a lovely lady called Shea," he informed her. "She wasn't able to come with me on this trip." Then he added. "Shea has her own charity, where she collects and provides food and clothing for the homeless people and families less fortunate in the community."

"Wow! That's impressive," said Muriel. "She must be an amazing lady."

"Yes, she is," Eli smiled as he thought of her. "Have you two ever travelled abroad?" he enquired.

"I went to Australia for a week," April informed him. "That was interesting." She laughed as she remembered something comical about her trip.

"Oh, yes," he encouraged. "How so?"

"I was attending a conference on disability and was staying at a very swanky hotel in the centre of Brisbane," she said. "I really enjoyed shopping there. The malls were huge compared to those I have seen here in New Zealand. I could have browsed all day and still not seen everything. So, I wanted to be out and about as much as possible to catch all the sights. Sometimes, I would go and sit in the large foyer near the entrance to our hotel. There, I could see the comings and goings of other guests and staff. It was fascinating. One day, a group of young people came in. I could tell that they hadn't come to stay. Apparently, they had come in to experience the atmosphere of successful living. Christians, who used the hotel foyer to meet and strategise their plans to form and build an organisation that would evangelise the world."

"Sounds like a plan to me," said Eli.

"Yes," April continued. "It was like they were there to embrace the initiative of other more successful people who were passing through, taking it for themselves and boldly proclaiming their rights to their own successful future."

"Wow. That sounds awesome," exclaimed Miriam.

"Who else did you meet," the rabbi wanted to know.

"There was the rich guy who sat reading his paper. But he was stuffy and ignorant," April replied. "He sat there like a wet piece of lettuce, pretending to read his newspaper but keeping a close eye on me."

"He probably thought you were there to steal his wallet," said Muriel. "If you had fluttered your eyelashes at him, he might have taken you to dinner."

"Yes," I agreed. "You missed your chance there, girl."

Everyone laughed. It is always fun being with April and Muriel. I never know where conversations will lead, and their humour is a real treat. April put her nose in the air and sniffed indignantly.

"I did say hello," she divulged. "But he never replied. I suppose he thought it was beneath him to speak to me."

"Well, if he is not going to speak to a nice girl like you, then he is not worth knowing," declared Miriam.

"That's right," the rabbi agreed. "It was, of course, his loss."

"I ignored him from then on," said April. "I wasn't going to waste my time and energy on a guy like that. No, I like fun people." Then her eyes brightened as another idea popped into her head. "On another subject, are you Jewish?" she asked the rabbi. And she turned her attention to him.

"Yes." The rabbi was pleased that she had recognised this. "Miriam and I are from Israel, but we now live next door to Robbie."

"Oh, that is so cool. We have a friend called Jody, who watches a woman on television," Muriel informed him. "Abby Jacobson. She is Jewish, I believe. Do you know about her?"

"Abby is my niece," the rabbi replied. "She was here recently to speak at some church functions. Her parents came too. They want to come back and travel around New Zealand."

"Wow! A small world, eh?" Muriel commented. "You kept that very quiet, Robbie. We rely on her to keep us up to date with all the gossip. But we only learn about it after it's all over. Why is that, Robbie?"

"Well, it's you two who think I'm the next Sherlock Holmes," I reminded them. "This is a lot to live up to. I can't remember everything. Besides, you have Jody to keep you well informed about coming Church events."

"So tell us all the gossip Robbie," Muriel said in very comical tones. "Have you been to lunch with Mike and Jeff lately? What kind of crime wave are you having back at home?"

"Oh, yes," Miriam quickly informed them. "She helped to catch the bad boyfriend of her sister. He is in jail now."

Muriel relaxed back in her seat, sporting one of those 'I knew it' looks and nodding her encouragement to learn more.

"We want to hear every detail," she declared. "So, you're right in the centre of the Police investigation then? Well, I'm not surprised." Then she indicated with her hands as she informed my friends. "If anything important is happening in Havenstream, you can be sure that Robbie is right there to assist." She laughed and turned to stare at me with a look that demanded more information

"That's why we call her Sherlock Holmes Two," April quickly added.

"So, tell us more about the Police action around here today," Eli encouraged. "They stopped us as we were driving into the housing area. Do we need to worry about leaving? We need to attend a meeting at the University this afternoon." He laughed as he talked.

April and Muriel excitedly began to relay the events at the house only a few yards away and why there was a police presence.

"The Armed Response Unit has been here all morning," said April. "They came into my yard and were standing at the fence with their guns drawn," she added, pointing towards the white house next door. "We could hear them calling to the people inside to come out. Finally, one of the guys appeared, and without saying a word, he knelt down in front of the police, put his hands behind his head and waited to be cuffed. It was fascinating."

"Yes, he knew what he had to do," Muriel confirmed. "But the wife refused to come out. She was yelling and screaming at the police. It took some time to get her to walk outside. We could hear her shouting abuse and her ongoing refusals to comply with the commands of the officers."

"The officer with the gun told us to stay inside," said April. "Safety first, I suppose. Well, it wouldn't be a good idea to be in the path of one of those dreaded bullets, eh?"

The rabbi looked at his watch and indicated to Eli that they must go. Miriam and I would stay and visit with April and Muriel until the two men returned from their meeting. I always enjoyed my time with these two comedians, and I could tell that Miriam was thrilled to be with us. She quickly got to work, made a batch of biscuits, and cleaned up the kitchen. April isn't the tidiest of people. She prefers watching television or going out rather than doing housework. Perhaps this is gossiping, but I just want to put you in the picture, so to speak. Anyway, soon the kitchen was sparkling clean. Yes, Miriam had it all in hand.

At about 3pm, the phone rang. It was my father. He sounded rather stressed. April turned on the speakerphone so that he could speak to us all.

"A lot is going on here," he said to April. "Angela's boyfriend is out of jail again, and has been very threatening. We have sent Angela to stay somewhere safe for the meantime, and we don't think that it is safe for Robbie to come back here. So, tell Robbie Jill and I are coming through and will take her to stay with some good people in Auckland."

Auckland! My spirit leapt with excitement and anticipation, causing my muscles to flinch involuntarily. The pain was immense, but oh, the joy to know that I would be able to see Pete, to have him so near. Absolutely, I would agree to this. My Pete, my love, my heart, lived there.

"Who?" I enquired, referring to where I would stay. Dad, of course, understood my shorthand speech.

"I talked to a lovely lady called Di Willis," he explained. "She is the Ministries Director of Elevate, the Christian organisation for people with disabilities. They also run that camp you have been telling me about." Then he laughed. "Or perhaps you would prefer to go and stay with Mrs Wrightson, the cook from the other camp. But you'd have to go on a diet. Your mother and I couldn't afford the food bills."

"Oh, no," Muriel quickly instructed him. "Don't send her to stay with Mrs Wrightson. Robbie would fade away to being a shadow of her former self. And we would end up having to do daily food deliveries."

"Yes," April chipped in. "I would be getting all those whining emails about how hungry she is and how she needs us to help her out. No, we just wouldn't be able to cope. Send her to stay with Di and Hugh. They will look after her well."

"Pete will look after me," I informed them all. "I think that he knows Di. So, he will come and take me out for a bite to eat."

"Poor Pete," Dad teased. "I hope you are going to pay. Pete is as poor as a church mouse. Not like you, Miss Money Bags. Okay, I will pick you up in about an hour. Oh, by the way, I have informed Samuel as to what is happening. He and Eli will be there shortly to pick up Miriam."

"Oh, no. We are keeping her," April informed him. "No more diet for me. Now that I've tasted her food, I need her here to cook for me."

"No, you can't have her as your cook," he replied. "We need her close by to be *our* cook, especially when she makes those awesome cakes. And you should taste her Lemon Meringue Pie. Super delicious!" And then he laughed. "Sometimes I sneak in there to have a cuppa and pie with Samuel. Don't tell Jill. She has me on some stupid diet."

"Well, in that case, she definitely must stay," Muriel stated in her most authoritative voice. "We want to sample one of her Lemon Meringue Pies." April nodded her agreement.

Half an hour later, the rabbi and Eli returned to pick Miriam up. They looked somewhat concerned when they talked about the situation back home with my sister and her boyfriend.

"How is it that people want to kill you, Robbie?" Eli wanted to know. "You must have secrets that you are not telling us."

"No, she's just nosey," April teased.

"But it is good for us that she is," Muriel chipped in. "We get to hear a lot of what's going on before others. She's our source, so to speak." Their faces were quite a picture, displaying an air of superior special knowledge.

"So, you're a gossip, Robbie," the rabbi laughed. "I would never have guessed. You look like you are such an innocent child."

"I don't tell them everything," I informed him. "There are things that I keep to myself. They just think that I tell them everything."

"Very wise," counselled Miriam. "There are some things that should not be shared. Robbie knows that. She's a good girl." Muriel and April looked over at me, disbelieving. I just sat back, showing a smug smile, secure that Miriam believed everything good about me, whether it was true or not.

As they left to go home, Eli said that he would email me about something he was planning and needed my help. I agreed and settled back to have a good gossip with the girls. Yet I felt an uneasiness deep within me. It was as though I was missing something important and couldn't remember the details. Yes, it was a weird feeling that I couldn't quite shake. But I didn't mention it to April and Muriel. They would have dismissed it as nerves and would tell me just to relax.

Dad arrived to pick me up around 4pm. He came in the van, bringing my electric wheelchair. I was thankful for that. Over the past couple of years, I had become more independent as I gained confidence with the motorised chair. So, now my life is less awkward and more relaxed.

"We are meeting your mother in Auckland," said Dad. "She is driving the car there, and we are leaving the van with Pete. This way, he won't have to push you in that heavy manual chair. And it will give you more independence when you are out and about."

"Cool. Thanks, Dad." Suddenly, I was so happy that my fears about spending time in places I was unfamiliar with, seemed to simply melt away. I had even forgotten about that uneasy feeling that had haunted me earlier. Anyway, I would often be with Pete, and he would ensure that nothing awful would happen to me.

We arrived at our destination safe and sound just over an hour and a half later. I was pleased to see that Mom and Pete were already here. Di came out to greet us.

"Hi Robbie," she said. "I'm so glad that you could come."

Di was chatty, kind and anxious to help get me into the house. I could tell she had an exceptional understanding of the difficulties that disabled people face. Back in the 1970s, Di and Hugh, her husband, and their friend Margie set up the Christian Fellowship for Disabled, now called Elevate. So, she's had over four decades of experience working to open opportunities and encourage people like Pete and me to come into a close relationship with God and to learn to live well in the bodies we have.

Meeting Di and Hugh, I knew I could trust them completely. Hugh is a soft-spoken man who works with Di to make the Elevate organisation run well. As I understand it, he loves the outdoors. Back in the 1970s, Hugh worked to clear bush and create tramping tracks so that people could safely walk and enjoy the nature in his district. He also wrote some books, showing where the tracks were and what wildlife walkers might find there. Later in life, Hugh lost his hearing and could no longer listen to the wonderful sounds of nature. Yet this did not deter him. He was always there when work needed to be done on the walking tracks. Others have helped him over the years, but his leadership was the key to the success of the nature walks. Hugh is a joy to know, just like his wife, Di.

We all had dinner together, enjoying the Shepherd's Pie that Mom had brought. Pete had taken a week's leave from his job, so we could spend some very needed time enjoying each other. It has always been difficult, living in different cities. Much of our relationship has been through letters and emails. Yet, now that Mom has accepted Pete as my boyfriend, it is so much easier to visit with him when he is able to come and see me.

Later, I settled in to get to know Di. It is so refreshing to be with someone who is happy to take the time to get to know everything about me, despite how I look and speak. Most people I meet are fine, but it still takes a little more effort for me to be understood well. Yet this was no problem for Di. She was eager to chat, letting me know that the things I had to say were important. She was also very excited to tell me about Elevate's national camp and invited me to come. I explained some things I had experienced at the other camp, and we laughed. Yes, I assured her, Pete and I would be coming to the Elevate camp later that year. Her eyes danced with joy as she told me how the Lord had helped many people through the ministry of Elevate. I could tell that this was what she wanted and prayed for me, yet I felt no pressure to change or try to become someone different from who I was. She was willing to wait for me to make that special discovery myself. Little did I know how near that experience was and what a difference it would make to my life.

Saturday morning had started a little chilly. However, by 10am, the sun's warm glow had melted the blustery winter blues away. Pete came to pick me up in the van, and I was looking forward to spending the day with him. First, we would go to the library, where he would drop off some books and pick up others to help him with his studies. I am very proud of my Pete. He is clever and has worked hard to carve out a career for himself. Many opportunities have opened up for him as he has gone forward, putting aside any concerns about his disabilities or inability to cope. He has such a beautiful smile and a great attitude about the future. He inspires me, and I am so fortunate to have him as my best friend.

I have always had such a fascination for libraries. The books have so many different colours and titles; I want to look at each one, imagine what the author might be like and how the story inside would influence me. Yes, I could spend hours in here. This was my happy place. So, while Pete combed through the shelves for the books on his list, I took on my own search and investigation. I drove my chair to the religious section. This was huge too. Scanning the shelves, I looked for an author I had heard of. No, I didn't see any of her work. However, I noted each name, even though it meant nothing to me. I was about to give up when a book caught my eye. The cover exploded with colour and personality. The book's title didn't matter to me at this point. It was the author that caught my attention: Eli Evans. I must have this book, I determined. I quickly put it in my lap and drove to where I would find Pete. He turned and picked up the books he had selected.

"All set to go now," he assured me. And I put the book I wanted on top of his books. He looked down carefully at the cover, and his eyebrows shot up. "Wow, heavy Christian stuff," he commented. Then he whistled, ever so quietly. "I didn't think you were too crazy about Christian authors."

"I just want to have a look at this one," I informed him. "Eli, the guy who is visiting the rabbi, wrote it. He wants me to help him with a project. So, I thought it would be a good idea to check out his previous works."

"Good thinking," he agreed. "You need to know what you are getting into."

We left the library, deciding to go to a nearby park. On the way, we called into a small café and bought some sandwiches and cake for our lunch. This time with Pete was so special, and I felt very content. It seemed that everything was working out well for us, that nothing could ever come between us now.

We arrived at the park and found a place to eat lunch. Not far away, other families were also picnicking and having fun. The sky was blue, and the sun was beaming down on us: a perfect day. Yet, in a matter of a moment, this would all change. I carry my bag very close to my body in my wheelchair. As far as I knew, no one could easily see it, and I didn't think much about it. But someone had spied that bag and had determined to steal it. He ran up to me and grabbed the bag. However, I had secured the handle to the chair. He found it was very difficult to detach from where I had fastened it. So, he produced a knife to cut the thick rope handles. By now, I also had hold of the bag and was not letting go. Suddenly, I felt a deep pain in my side as he plunged the knife into me. My body flinched with the pain. I became weak and now had no power to hold myself up, so I stopped struggling, and he got away. Hearing Pete's cries for help, people came running and gathered around me. A man lifted me out of my wheelchair, gently putting me on the ground. Others tried to stop the flow of blood with whatever they could.

It was at this time that my reality began to change. I was watching everything from outside my physical body. Surveying my surroundings, I saw a scared young man running from the scene. It was bizarre because I could feel his panic. He ran this way and that, not knowing where to go, or what he should do. In his hand was a bloody knife. Suddenly, he looked down at the knife, and as he remembered, the gravity of his crime overcame him. Quickly, he found a bush and threw it underneath the leaves. Then he ran as fast as possible to his regular hideout, a shed behind some shops.

As for me, I felt very peaceful and detached from what was happening in the park. Yes, it seemed that I had been removed from that injured body below. Presently, I heard someone call my name. I turned and saw the same angel from the day before, who had been standing behind Eli as he prayed for the family overseas.

"The King has sent for you," he revealed. "You must come with me." His eyes and manner were full of joyful expectation and engulfed me with a warmth that I can't adequately explain. All I can say is that it touched every part of me, both inside and out, strengthening and extending my abilities in a way they had never been.

Eagerly, I walked over to join him. There was no memory of the pain of what had happened in the park only a short time ago. I just wanted to be where he was taking me. In less than a blink of an eye, my surroundings changed, and I was standing inside an expansive library. The shelves were wall to wall, full of books, papers, scrolls and movies. The atmosphere was electric. It was as though the books were speaking to me, beckoning… no, begging me to read their stories. As I listened, my whole being was drawn into the intricate webs of many lives. When people tell you that if the walls had ears and could talk, they would have a great deal to say, believe them.

They surely do. Everything we utter, whether good or bad, stays in the universe, can be recalled and written in our own personal biographies in this fantastic place where stories are so important. I didn't yet know why I was here in this fascinating place, but I was excited and eager to see what would happen next. There was an all-encompassing love in this place that created life, bringing light and understanding. Yes, I would enjoy my time in this library.

CHAPTER SIX

Surveying the library shelves, I became aware of a picture of someone I recognised. It was Jason Boyd, President of Morgandy, a nation in crisis. Over recent months, a great deal had been written and said about him, both good and bad. Many loved him. To them, he was like a saviour, a guru, the pied piper who was promising the best of life to every resident of the tiny realm in the Caribbean. Others hated him with a passion and would work tirelessly to rid their country of his influence. His image was on the front cover of a book, and the author was none other than my friend Eli Evans. *Well,* I thought. *I must check this out.* So, I walked over and picked up the book—the title, 'Presidential: The King's Choice'. As I quickly thumbed through the pages, I got the impression that Eli believed that Mr Boyd was the only person who could lead the nation into a time of health and prosperity for the future. And now, this was interesting: My name was in the credits as a researcher for the book. *So, this was the work that he wants me to help him with,* I mused.

For some moments, I concentrated on the title of the book. Who was this king that Eli was referring to here? I had heard historians use the term *king-maker* mentioned regarding a person who would be in a top position to open the way to promote a particular person into leadership. But this was a combination of Christianity and political theory. Eli explains it as a prophetic message from God. Yes, this would be interesting for me to look into and explore. Quickly, I opened the pages. The words seemed to jump off the pages as they encouraged me to read Eli's story.

Well, Eli certainly is a great writer. In life-giving words, he had taken the time to paint a very vibrant picture from Bible stories, particularly the Gospels, of the day that Jesus Christ died on the cross. It was very poignant, using his own particular style and imagery and greatly affected me. Eli begins by explaining that during his three years of ministry, Jesus had touched many lives uniquely.

Yet it was his claim to a close relationship with God that most upset the Jewish leaders and made them so angry. He had called God his father and claimed he and his father were one. This would make him equal with God, the Creator. In his Ministry, he healed the sick, miraculously fed thousands with very little food available and raised the dead. Thus, he showed such a power and ability that the people had never seen before. When asked about these things, he said that he only did what he saw his father doing. Then he denounced the priests and the scribes for their failure to live worthily before God. These religious leaders were very prominent in the Jewish community and did not want to be called out by some unknown preacher from Galilee. They were also envious of that special relationship he had with his father God. Because of this special connection, he was able to help people who came to him. The priests and the scribes could not do these things. Thus, they felt that their influence with the common people in the community had been diminished. So, they planned to get rid of Jesus. But how would they do it? The men determined that by using small unruly crowds who would do their bidding, they could stir up negative rumours, embellishing the stories and then make their Roman rulers aware of the situation. It sounded like a good plan. This way, they would be able to get the job done without getting their own hands dirty. In the opening chapter, Eli sets the scene around the crucifixion.

The stage is set during the week that Passover would be celebrated. Jesus was becoming a very popular preacher travelling around the countryside. So, the Jewish leaders developed a plan. Joining with the scribes, they went to Pontius Pilate, the ruling Roman Governor of Judaea. The men told Pilate that Jesus was calling himself a king and was inciting the common people to rise up against the present ruling government. This way, Pilate would be responsible for dealing with him, and the religious men would not be held responsible for his death. It was Judas Iscariot, one of Jesus' twelve disciples, who betrayed him, enabling the arrest. But Jesus did not resist his arrest, although he did pause to heal the ear of one of the soldiers that had been cut off with a sword. So, not even an arrest or being under guard could prevent Him from doing miracles.

As Jesus stood in the Praetorium, or Governor's Palace, Pilate asked him if he was, in fact, a king. Jesus replied that he was, but that his kingdom was not of this world. He further explains to Pilate that if his kingdom were of this world, his servants would have been fighting to keep him from being handed over to the Jewish leaders to be killed.

"So, you are a king?" Pilate asked for further definable clarification of Jesus' status that would prove that he had heard correctly. Jesus again confirmed that he was a king and that he had come to earth to bring truth to a world where lies and deceit reign. "What is truth?" Pilate asked, literally spitting out the words and then left the room without waiting for an answer.

Yet there must have been something about Jesus that resonated with Pilate because he did not believe that Jesus had done anything horrifying enough to be convicted of any crime or execution. He would have heard the chatter about Jesus, even the guards in discussion, saying, "Never have we heard a man speak like this one does." It was certainly something that he had to take time to consider. His plan, at this point, was to whip him mercilessly, showing the onlookers that he had indeed punished the man and then let him go. However, those around him continued to pressure him to put Jesus to death. Pilate was becoming quite frustrated. It was a great dilemma for him. What should he do? He was betwixt a rock and a hard place. Even his wife warned him not to get involved with this issue. She'd had a dream about Jesus that affected her very deeply. So, he went back to talk again to Jesus, reminding him that he had the authority to either crucify him, or release him. Jesus, on the other hand, was not intimidated by this and told Pilate that he had no authority over him except that which God gave him. Jesus also assures Pilate that for this reason, the sin and guilt of the man who handed him over, Caiaphas, the High Priest, was greater than his own. Again, Pilate tried to stop the crucifixion, but in the end, he bowed to pressure and Jesus was put to death on the cross.

Above his head, and nailed to the cross, was an inscription, stating that Jesus was *King of The Jews*. Eli explains that at this time, it was the custom that when a man was crucified, his crimes were written in gypsum letters and displayed on a rough board for all to see. Perhaps at first glance, this may not appear of great importance. After all, he was a Jewish man and had purposely called out the religious leaders. Before his arrest, he had openly declared that they were hypocrites and whitewashed tombs, looking beautiful on the outside, but on the inside, they were full of dead man's bones and everything unclean. This is just a small portion of how he described them in the Gospel accounts. But in fact, those words had in the end, sealed his fate, sending him to Pilate and his death by a cruel crucifixion.

These words, *King of The Jews,* were written in the three languages of that province. It sent a clear message to everyone who dared to rise against the ruling classes in that area. So, no matter which group they belonged to, they would see this as a warning to stay within the bounds of what was considered good behaviour. The words first appeared in Latin. This was the official language of the Roman Empire and represented government, power and conquest. Eli explains that many scholars believe that Pilate had personally dictated the words to his chief centurion in charge of executions. Pilate himself was multi-lingual, able to speak at least three languages, Latin, Greek and Aramaic. Eli says that some scholars believe this because, in Mathew's gospel, he discusses the fate of Jesus with the chief priests, elders and onlookers. Their argument was that it was likely these people would not have understood Latin, and Pilate did not speak Hebrew. Also, his Greek would have been far better than his Aramaic. So, Greek would have been his preferred choice of language to confer with the men about the situation. In putting the inscription in Latin, it is likely that Pilate was sending a clear message to the community, showing them that justice would be swift and violent to those who would not be reigned in. He sought to remind them that they and much of the known world at that time, were subject to Roman Law, and they had no authority to rule in their own right.

As I read through the pages of Eli's book, I found it absolutely fascinating to understand what happened next. The religious leadership then tried to persuade Pilate to alter the inscription, changing it from *King of The Jews* to *I Am the King of The Jews*. This would change the perception of what the sentence was saying, and its tone. The men did not want people thinking that Jesus was actually a person of great significance in the Jewish community. It would make them conspirators in the death of an important public figure. This way, they are just dealing with a largely unknown agitator who has aspirations to become king of the Jews. Now, some commentators believe that Pilate was a weak man, a puppet of Caesar. And this may have been true in some respect. However, when it came to the Jewish High Priest and his supporters, Pilate would stand firm and resolute in his decision.

"What I have written, I have written," he told the men, indicating that he would not change his mind. Pilate knew, and it irritated him that the men were trying to manipulate him. This was so they could get a certain outcome without taking any responsibility. After Jesus was publicly whipped and before he was led away to his death, Pilate again gave the people the opportunity to save his life.

A few months ago, Mom and I watched an interesting video discussing this. A historian had a theory of what was probably happening here. He said that there were two types of people in attendance. Firstly, there were those who saw him do miracles and heard his teachings. These were disciples. They wept as they watched the cruelty of the soldiers. However, none of them raised their voices in his defence. Then there was another crowd, agitators, who were very vocal, screaming out for Jesus to be crucified. The historian in the video believed that these people had possibly been brought in from Judaea, hired to support the religious leaders in attaining their desired result. It was an interesting concept, and since then, every now and again, I have briefly looked at some of the research for myself.

Jesus suffered a cruel death that day on the cross between two thieves. Large nails pierced his wrists and ankles, forcing him to try to hold himself up to breathe. He would not have any skin, or muscle still on his back. The forty lashes with the whip left his body bare of any covering except the flowing blood from every wound. Then the soldiers fashioned a crown made of thorns and roughly placed it on his head. Each barb was driven deeply into his skull, causing extreme pain and releasing blood and fluid. By this time, he was unrecognisable. The soldiers cast lots for his robe. People came to observe him as he was dying on that cross. They scorned and sneered.

"Look," they said, "He could save others, but he couldn't save himself."

This was not the way a king should be treated. Neither was it how a man who only brought good things to society should end his life. In his three short years of ministry, he ended the suffering of many people, making their lives better. Yet his own life was ended with incredible torture, agony and trauma. To those looking on, this appeared to be the end of him. Yet this was not so. Three days later, the tomb was found to be open, the soldiers who had been charged with keeping the tomb secured were nowhere in sight, and Jesus was gone. The grave clothes he had been wrapped in were folded neatly on the slab where he had laid. During the next forty days, over five hundred people saw him walking, talking and doing normal things after his death. Eli asserts that this alone proves that he is set apart from any other human. Many have given their lives for a cause, but only one man has ever come back to cook breakfast for his disciples. So, it was clear to me now that the king Eli was referring to was his Lord Jesus, to whom he had devoted his life. Today Eli is very vocal about how he lives a different life. He says that his life principles come directly from the Bible and that he has a close relationship with Jesus, his Saviour and King.

So, this is where Eli begins his story about Jason Boyd, who he believed was the King's choice for President of the tiny nation of Morgandy. As Eli looked at the events leading up to the elections, he began to get a clear sense that something unusual, something unique was about to happen. Two almighty cosmic armies, good and evil, were about to face off in battle for control of the world, and the skirmishes would begin in Morgandy with the coming election. No one could even conceive of the great terror ahead that would change and challenge the world so completely.

I was standing there, pondering the significance of all these things, when I became aware of someone nearby, watching me. Quickly, I turned, and my breath was literally taken away as I beheld the inexplicable beauty of the man before me. It was like He had been placed inside a rainbow, and the colours were spectacularly moulded into His being. Therefore, not only could I see the picturesque view around Him, but the colours also emanated from within Him. It seemed that the rays of light and shade were an integral part of Him. As He extended His hand to me, I couldn't help but notice the scars on His wrists. I also studied His face, and there I witnessed the many severe injuries on His head. Little telltale scars all over his forehead became the focus of my attention. Suddenly, my thoughts went back to Jesus and his death on the cross. Before His crucifixion, the soldiers had made fun of Him and had created a crown of thorns to mockingly signify His royal status. Yes, I was standing in the presence of the King that Eli was talking about in his book. He was also the man from the garden whom I had met several years ago when I had that terrible accident. Quickly, I dropped to my knees and knelt in silent worship. There were no words that would be enough. Gently, He lifted me to my feet, and for a moment, He drew me to Him with His eyes.

"Come, walk with me," He urged. His voice reminded me of the crashing sound of waves in the ocean that embrace the shores on a sunny day. "There is such a lot for you to see," He told me. "And there is much more for you to be." Then He gently turned me in the direction that we should walk. "I want you to meet some of my friends," He said. "They will help you to understand who you are and what I have for you in your future. Don't just read about me, Robbie, or treat me as just an interesting character in history. As you can see, I am real, alive. I have thoughts, feelings, structure, purpose, and ability. See, I have already begun to open my unique treasury to you. Here, you are on assignment, where you will discover the power of story. Sometimes the story will be interweaved with your own; at other times, not. But you will know the difference. When you need me, and you will, just talk to me. I will answer you, perhaps in ways that may surprise you. But you will know for sure that it is me."

The sun's energy pressed upon me with a comforting warmth, reflecting the joy emanating from the King's heart. I knew He wanted me to visit one of His favourite places, but I didn't know yet where we were going.

Presently, we arrived at a church building. It was small, the shape of a square box, made of timber and painted white. It was just like buildings in stories about the wild west on television. I looked around and laughed to myself. I enjoy watching movies set in that period; the scene was so familiar and comforting. Filmmakers seem to capture the times and the ambience so well. *Hollywood has come to Heaven*, I thought. And the joy of expectation bubbled up within me, whipping my enquiring mind into a storm of determined desire to investigate further.

"Hollywood hasn't come to Heaven, Robbie," the King advised me. "No, it is the other way around. I have taken Heaven to Hollywood. Yes, I have many close friends who live and work there, and they work with me to bring good stories that comfort, encourage and inspire people to do great things. You have seen many of those valuable stories. And I know that some of them have touched your heart very deeply.

"Oh, yes," I concurred. "There are movies that I watch again and again."

"Yes, well, I am the real Executive Producer of those shows because I planted the desire in the heart of those I have called to initiate the project. Then I put an idea into another person's mind, giving them an impression of how to create the story. The actors are chosen through my counsel. It isn't just by chance that the film comes together well. The Spirit of Promise and Helper is always there to assist."

As we walked towards the church, He put His arm around my shoulders. It was a very tender moment, and I felt incredibly happy.

"When I returned to be with my Father," he explained, "the Spirit of Promise was sent to comfort, teach and direct the steps of people who are willing to listen and take advice. He also convicts people, showing them that they are walking the wrong path for their lives. His greatest joy is to show them the Father's heart and his best life for them. This is the decision that you have to make, Robbie. You have free choice. So, you need to look at the pathway you are currently walking alone and choose whether you stay on it or want to be a part of my world."

I nodded. Yes, I understood.

"It was you on that cross, wasn't it?" I said.

His eyes drew me nearer, showing me the love that kept his heart beating.

"I was," He concurred. "It was a painfully difficult thing for me to do. No one else could take my place. But I am not there now. If you look closely at the stories in the Bible, they will tell you about me, my Father and the Spirit of Promise."

"Where is your Father?" I wanted to know.

"You will meet Him soon." His words were quiet and reflective. "But as I said to my disciples, my Father and I are as one person. Because you have seen me, you have already seen my Father."

Well, that wasn't really what I wanted to hear. I like to see everything. Yet I did understand what He was saying, and I could accept it, for now. We walked up the steps of the old church, and the door swung open. Suddenly, I had to turn away and shield my eyes. The light was so bright that I found it difficult to focus. The King caught me as I stumbled through the doorway. His hold was strong and reassuring, capturing me in a way I had never experienced before.

"This is a very special place, Robbie," he said. "You know it as a church, perhaps a little country church. And, on any given day, you could drive by in your wheelchair without even giving it much thought. But people come here for many reasons; some to sit in solitude, others to draw near and examine their own lives because they believe that they should talk to someone bigger and wiser than themselves. Some call out to Father God, even though they don't actually know Him. Yet they firmly believe that He hears them. And He does. We all do. We hear every prayer and care about each situation that they face. Life is extremely challenging for some, Robbie. Actually, you have had a taste of it this week at home. Angela will never tell you, but she has been mercilessly beaten several times. Her jaw has been broken, as well as several ribs and one of her wrists. There are many bruises all over her body. He has even burned her with his cigarettes. His brutality is too horrifying to describe fully. I'm telling you just a small part of what she has endured. She is a broken woman, Robbie, and she needs your support, even your help. You are strong enough and have the compassion to do this, for I have given you the ability."

His words took my breath away, and for some moments, I could scarcely take it all in. Of course, I already knew that the boyfriend had done awful things to her. It had been evident to us all when she arrived home. Nonetheless, it was difficult to hear the exact details. Yes, He could depend on me to help and support her.

Looking around the little church, I was struck by the beauty of its interior. The walls were covered with colourful precious stones. They seemed to be cut and fitted together perfectly. As many fingers of the radiant sunshine rested on them, their reflections were worked into a marvellous rainbow that covered almost the entire interior of the building.

"These precious stones are the master artist's impression of those who have greatly suffered," He said. "A picture of people who have lived fractured lives and endured great suffering and adversity in a broken world. While you are here, I want you to meet these people for yourself. I can see you are already curious." And He laughed. "Often, I see your brain running in overtime mode to try to work out the puzzling things that bamboozle you," He teased. "I would say that you are unique. But no. We purposely made you like that. We do it all the time. Now, you need to discover for yourself what is inside of you. As you branch out, you will become more confident and want to go further, trying other new things. You may not always be successful, but you will, in any event, increase your determination to find your way to a triumphant result."

I looked away for only a moment. Lost in my thoughts, I tried to absorb everything the King had said. Then the questions came tumbling into my mind, so, I turned again to find out more from Him. But He was gone. In His place was the angel that I had met before. It was strange. I now knew his name. He was called Vitus, which means life. He extended his hand and said that I must come with him.

"Where are you taking me?" I asked. And we began walking. For a few moments, he looked over at me with a mischievous grin.

"I think you are going to be happy," he said. "We are going to another library so that you can see some more books and meet two intriguing friends of mine. But I'll be leaving you at the entrance. Your friend Eli has asked the King to send his angels to watch over you as you sleep in the hospital."

A feeling of well-being went right through me when I heard him mention Eli. Suddenly, I wanted to be assured that all my friends were safe and okay. Yet, at the same time, I knew they were, and I could relax.

"Please tell him that I am okay," I responded. "You know how he worries when his friends are in a crisis."

"I will give him a hug for you," he assured me.

"Will he know that it is from me?"

"Oh, yes," he assured me. "I will let him know that you sent it."

We walked together a little further, and then he disappeared.

CHAPTER SEVEN

Arriving at a large old-fashioned homestead, the beauty of the surrounding land overwhelmed me. The gardens were far beyond anything I had ever seen on earth. And the perfumes were so engaging. I cannot describe them except that they were perfectly natural and stirred my spirit to dance with delight. No, these fragrances had certainly not been manufactured in a chemical lab. As I looked at each particular flower, it seemed to become animated, rising to greet me, filling me with great strength and anticipation. Then I looked further but could not detect where the garden ended.

The house itself was fascinating. It was made of natural cedar wood and had carved exterior walls which were highly polished. I had never seen anything like it before. Momentarily, I wondered who lived there. Stepping inside, I was overwhelmed by the power of story. I was made aware of how, through impossible odds, many nations were born, and communities were built. People stood tall in the struggle for victory, both in public battles and personal hardships in their private lives, men and women of purpose and determination. Yes, I was in another library.

Quickly, I scanned the shelves to see what titles I knew or was interested in. Some were chronicles of law stories, and others that attracted my eye were historical accounts of famous political figures. However, I was also astonished to see Eli's book, *Presidential: The King's Choice* sitting on a nearby table. Some pages were partially open, indicating that someone had been reading them. Turning to my right, I saw a small sitting room area with comfortable armchairs and a coffee table. On it was a pile of books waiting to be read. Two elderly statesmen sat discussing world events, quietly commenting on each development as they saw them happen on earth. It was as though a huge television screen was in front of them. But there was no need for such a device here. When the friends wanted to see an event, a space opened up in front of them, and a live video appeared.

I know that it may seem somewhat inadequate in my description, but this is the only way I can tell you so that you will understand. It was fascinating to see, yet it didn't seem strange or unusual to me.

I looked closer to see what they were watching. The scene was of President Jason Boyd of the tiny nation of Morgandy. He was on the lawn of his home, Tabor Palace, hosting a news conference to set out his plans for the future in his endeavour to grab the top job in the government. The next seven months would be pivotal to advance in his aspirations. Yes, he would again embark on a race to become President of Morgandy for the next four years. His absolute conviction was that he was not just the best man but the *only* man for that job. He made that clear to everyone. He wasted no time in letting people know that there was no one else who could do a better job than he. I was fascinated by what I was hearing.

However, the race to take residence in Tabor Palace could be much tougher for him this time. There was severe racial and social unrest, and constant criticism, mainly in the media, dogged his every step. His enemies were so many and seemed to pop up on every side. Their relentless efforts to ruin him were always in public so the whole world could witness it. But amazingly, he pushed on with business as usual, strong and resolute. *But why was this?* I wondered. Why was he so driven to be the President of this little nation? And where does he get the strength to prepare to do a third term of office? The previous eight years had been absolutely horrific. Yet he had taken it all in his stride, and the stress hadn't seemed to bother him. Maybe if I looked closer, I could perhaps glean some vital information that would give me the answers to these questions.

I watched as President Boyd seemed very upbeat, recounting all the successes of his presidency to the journalists before him. He believed that his administration had taken significant strides in lifting the economy in the past eight years, providing more employment opportunities, especially for the destitute in the community and changing healthcare, making it more affordable. He was thrilled to inform the world that everything was on track for a promising future in Morgandy. He also talked about what he had done in other countries. His chest puffed out with pride as he gave his own version of his successes. This was in keeping with his own particular style of self-esteem. He boasted about his exploits and what he planned for the future of Morgandy. I smiled to myself as he announced to the world that he had done a very, very good job and that no one could have done it better.

For some time, the Press sat quietly listening. It seemed to me that they were fascinated and genuinely interested in what the President had to say. But I was mistaken; this was just the calm before the storm. Taking the opportunity in a moment of silence, one of the journalists spoke up and accused President Boyd of not doing enough to help the growing racial tensions in all areas of the nation and demanded to know what the President was going to do to fix it. This seemed to indicate to others that it was time to join in. Soon they were all talking over each other, calling out questions and attempting to have their say. Not even Mr Boyd could be heard. He tried to gain control, holding his hand up as a sign for them to stop and listen. But nothing changed. His annoyance was clear as he turned to leave. Ignoring the crazy, out-of-control emotion, he just walked away. It was quite extraordinary. Those in the syndicated Press looked more like an unruly mob as they tried to follow him. Some attempted to thrust microphones in his face to get any sort of statement. President Boyd did not speak. Quickly, he retreated into the safety of the Palace. He would not be seen again today. Although the sun shone brilliantly upon the vast lawns and gardens, in the distance, I could see angry storm clouds swirling, waiting for the opportunity to strike.

As the two friends watched this live news clip, they exchanged glances and smiled. They may have come from somewhat different family backgrounds, and their approach to politics may have differed, but in this place, they were one in mind and spirit in this matter.

"Who is on the Lord's side?" one man asked. "There is so much dissension, dysfunction and anger. How can this man govern this nation? I have never before seen such opposition."

"Yes, these are difficult times," commented the other as they watched each fascinating event unfold before their eyes. "But we know that the King has appointed and equipped this man for this particular position in this momentous time. He has given him a solid inner constitution to enable him to stand strong against his enemies."

"I know," laughed the first gentleman. "Isn't it amazing?! He believes completely in his own ability to make our nation great in the eyes of the wider world. And he handles his detractors well, giving them back as good as he gets. But I wish he wouldn't do so many of those little messages on the internet. They only seem to drive people crazy."

"I have heard them called *TWEETS*," said his friend. "I agree. He writes so many. We didn't have them in our day. We didn't need them. On the other hand, as the King has explained, although he is imperfect, yet he still fits perfectly to be President for this particular time."

So, who were these two esteemed gentlemen who took such interest in the politics of this little nation of Morgandy? One I recognised right away from his picture in the history books. It was Jim Lazenby. I knew it was him because he has such distinctive facial features that it could be none other.

Mr Lazenby was a past President of Morgandy, holding this office in the mid-nineteenth century. Eli had also touched on several aspects of his life in his latest book about President Boyd. These things I find so fascinating. Researching is my thing. For instance, I can tell you that Mr Lazenby was born in a small village in the north country, but when he was eight years old, the family travelled by boat to the United States of America and lived on the frontier, mainly in Indiana. His family was impoverished and unable to provide many of life's necessities for the lad. When he was ten years old, his mother died. Life was difficult in those days, helping out where he could. In his autobiography, he recalls that as a family, they lived in a very wild area of the country, with many bears and other animals in the woods. This meant that education wasn't available to him. So, he was self-educated. That being said, and despite his circumstances, some years later, when he returned to Morgandy, he became a most sought-after and successful lawyer. His autobiography states further that he didn't know much when he came of age. Yet, somehow, he could read, write and cypher, but no more than that. Now, that wasn't exactly true. Mr Lazenby was, in fact, a very clever man. History records show that he had a remarkable ability to assess the needs of the people in his nation and used his wisdom to change lives for the good. He moved into politics, and in 1843, he ran for Senator against a seasoned politician, though narrowly losing the election. However, during the debates, people saw his worth, and he won the nomination for President of Morgandy in 1856. His tremendous influence has been the strength, security and stability upon which subsequent governments of Morgandy and the people have stood. I felt privileged to be here with him and his friend.

The other gentleman was Tom Glass, also a past President of Morgandy. Presently, he turned to his friend, Jim and smiled warmly.

"We have a guest, Jim," he said cheerfully, "And she knows something about our lives and work. Good morning, Miss Robbie." His words of acknowledgement brought warmth to my heart, and he seemed to know where my interests lay.

"Good morning, Mr President," I replied. Then turning to Mr Lazenby, I made sure to acknowledge him also. "Good morning to you too, Mr President. I am honoured to meet you both."

Mr Lazenby invited me to sit with them so they could chat with me. His eyes were full of kindness and an interest in teaching me.

"Here, we honour the King only," he instructed me. "He is our greatest joy; our Champion. And He can be yours as well. This is why you are here today."

"Yes, we saw that young man stab you," disclosed Mr Glass. "He is very regretful now about what he has done. He is going to talk to his mama. Yes," he nodded in agreement with his own thoughts. "She is a good woman. She will know what to do and help him. And you can help him too."

I remember doing a particular study about Tom Glass when I was at College. I chose him because he was one of the principal people who drafted and changed Morgandy's Constitution to what it is today. Born in 1743 in the American Colonies, Mr Glass' father was a planter and surveyor, owning 5,000 acres. His mother was from the Reed family, with high social standing. Her family believed that they were descended from English and Scottish royalty. So, he was brought up differently than Mr Lazenby.

At the age of nine, young Tom began formal studies in mathematics and science at a private school under the tuition of a scholar called Mr Fife. He prospered academically and was considered the highest achiever in the school. So, as a young man, no one was surprised when Tom achieved great things at College. During his lifetime, he was awarded four honorary degrees and was successful in everything he did. In his early twenties, Mr Glass travelled to Morgandy and settled in the city of Monroe. This was where he began to carve out his political career.

Although he made some speeches as a politician, Mr Glass was shy and did not like this part of his work. Yet, history has recorded that he contributed skilfully with the pen. Not only did he draft and was a principal writer of the country's most important laws, but he also co-founded the Freedom Party, believing that the nation's political power should have only a limited role in the lives of its citizens. There were other things, though, that I found questionable about his life. He was sometimes dishonest in his dealings with people, which made him many enemies. Yet his political career survived, and ultimately, he was recorded in history as one of Morgandy's greatest politicians.

As I now sat beside President Glass, many questions flooded my mind. My most pressing thought was concerning how he got to be living here. It was becoming clear that I was visiting a heavenly place where God lives. So, if this was true, and he was a man who had done so many things that would be called *unchristian* by those in the church, how is it that I find him here? It surprised me that a man who had done so much good for his country, could also have this other life that was so opposed to the community standards of the day. Just then, he touched my arm to gain my attention.

"It's true," he confessed. "I did all those things you read about in your study. I was that man. God's pure love flooded my heart and drew me out of the dark pit of deception. That day my life changed. You have met the King, and you have seen many of His attributes and abilities. The truth, Robbie, is that until you open your heart and look into His heart, you will never be whole. There is so much more for you to learn and to experience."

"Yes," Mr Lazenby chipped in. "The King has given you the gift of life, Robbie. Take that gift, hold it close, give it your lifeblood and then release it into the world and allow it to take flight. You have the opportunity to influence and help to change many lives for the good. Consider the young man who stabbed you. He needs your understanding and forgiveness so that he can heal too."

"He hurt me," I complained. "You know that he stabbed me, stole my money and then ran away, leaving me to die. Why should I forgive him?"

"Because if you don't, you will never be able to move on," said Mr Lazenby. "And if you can't move forward with your life, you will never reach the greatest goals and abilities that are in your future. Besides, you can give him a wonderful gift. I think he needs that gift."

"I don't know if I want to." Quickly, I turned away because I could no longer look the two men in the eye. Yes, and I was stumbling over every word. I did feel guilty at that moment, but greater was the hurt that the memory facilitated to keep me in the prison of unforgiveness. Hot tears swirled inside my pain, unsettling my equilibrium, but I fought against the impulse to give in with all my strength. While I knew that I should, at this moment, there was still no way I could simply give in.

"We have no pity parties here, Robbie." Mr Glass put his hand on my shoulder and gently encouraged me to turn so that we were looking eye to eye. "This is a decision that only you can make. No one is going to twist your arm. But while you are here, you have the opportunity to see his story. Would you like to take this journey?"

I nodded and sat back to wait for what might be coming next. Again, a scene as in a video opened up in front of me. This time, I saw a wee boy, no more than three years old, playing with a toy tractor in the family room of his house.

"Vroom, vroom, vroom," he vocalised, attempting to make the distinctive sound of the tractor.

Nearby, his stepdad sat watching television and drinking beer. I could tell that he had devoured quite a few because there were squashed empty cans all over the floor. Each time he finished his drink, he crushed the container with his hand and tossed it on the floor. Briefly, he looked over at the boy and then took another glug of his beer. He seemed to be somewhat agitated and tapped his fingers on the arm of his chair. Then he turned again to look at the boy.

"Put that tractor away," he demanded.

"But I want to play with it," wailed the boy.

"Don't you talk back to me!" shouted the man. "Put that thing away right now!" And he lifted his fist to show that he meant business. Seeing this, the boy cowered away from him, getting as low as he could towards the floor. Then he began to cry; not too loudly, in case he made things worse. Suddenly, the man totally lost his cool. He stood up and walked quickly over to the boy, picked him up and threw him with great force against the wall. The wee lad crumpled to the floor and lay there silent and motionless. This sight was absolutely horrendous. I could hardly believe what I was seeing. At that very moment, the boy's mother appeared, scooped him into her arms and cradled him close to her heart. She kissed his forehead gently and whispered his name. Presently, she looked up at her husband but didn't speak. No, it would not have been a good idea to do that. Past experiences of beatings, and seeing her son punished for little or no wrongdoings at all, told her that she must stay silent for now. The man went and sat down heavily into his chair, picked up another can, opened it and took a swig.

"I'll need more beer soon," he mumbled.

Cradling her son, the woman understood that he was telling her she must go to the liquor store for him, so she turned to leave the room.

"Let's go for a walk," she said to the boy, and the scene vanished from before my eyes. In all honesty, my emotions were now in a mess. I love children, and yes, I was right there in the moment. My own body cried out with the same terror and desperation that he was experiencing. And then I became furious. *This evil man needs to be arrested and put away forever*, I barked inwardly. *How will that little boy survive?* Every time I closed my eyes, scenes of the child suffering that abuse filled my mind, and I was becoming quite distressed. Suddenly, I felt the tears fill my eyes and the sobs well up in my throat. I needed to pull myself together.

"Don't hold back, Robbie," Mr Lazenby counselled me. "Let your heart feel his pain. Most people don't understand because he doesn't speak about it. But he and his mama have been through such tragedy. From a very early age, starting when he was only a baby, his stepfather abused him. I can tell you that his body has been covered in bruises from beatings and burns from stubbed-out cigarettes."

"There is more to this story that you need to know, Robbie, but not yet," said Mr Glass. "Other adventures await your attention. We will say goodbye for now so you can explore our library further."

CHAPTER EIGHT

Looking around at the publications this great library held, several of the books again became quite animated. Beating hearts of stories as yet unread were calling to me. They were anxious to have my attention and would not allow me to ignore them.

"Robbie, Robbie," they cried out. "Please don't pass me by. I am strength. Choose my hope. Call on my comfort. Reach out for my joy."

So, excusing myself from the two men, I got up and began to walk past each shelf. What should I choose? They all looked so good. Finally, a particular book caught my eye. It seemed to smile at me. Yes, I must look further. With care, I picked up the tattered, old hardback publication and looked closely at its cover. It was plain to me that many people in times past, perhaps connected by family tradition, had handled it, treasured it, and devoured each word until the book had finally fallen apart. The cover that had once been a rich brown was now a faded yellow colour, and I could only just make out the words "Holy Bible" that had once been written in distinctive gold lettering.

Suddenly, a middle-aged woman, perhaps in her late forties, came into view. Her name was Reinette Evans-Davies, and the date was October 5, 2019. I witnessed her sitting at the kitchen table with her mother, Estelle Evans. The pair were looking closely at the old Bible, which had been in the family for nearly two centuries. This was the day that Estelle would officially pass the precious family heirloom to her daughter. Both women felt a deep sadness as they considered the changes that were coming soon to their lives. Estelle, who had recently been diagnosed with the beginnings of dementia, had decided to sell up and move into an elderly facility. She knew that in time she would not be able to look after herself, and she did not want to put that responsibility on her daughter's shoulders. A large

'For Sale' sign stood boldly on the front lawn of the family home, indicating that future plans were being formulated quickly.

As Reinette thumbed through the pages of the old Bible, pictures of her childhood flooded her mind. Many were happy days; others were not. She smiled to herself as she recalled several family events and people who brought her such joy when they came to visit. At that moment, Eli's face came into view, and my happiness glands responded with a big smile. It was so good to see him again, even if only in a type of hologram.

"Do you remember when Uncle Eli came to visit, and we went to the Spy Museum?" Reinette asked her mother. Her laughter was so infectious, and the joy of that particular memory sparked a fire of details almost forgotten in Estelle's mind. She turned to her daughter and gave a response rarely seen these days.

"Yes," she replied. "You were thirteen and very pedantic about what you did and didn't like. Well, when Eli announced that he was going to dress up as a detective to visit the Museum, you were not happy and refused to go with us. You said that you didn't want to be seen in public with a crazy person. But Eli was determined to get you to change your mind. And he did." Estelle was pleased with herself that she had remembered. "I can still see the outfit that he wore," she said. "He looked every bit like the famous man, Sherlock Holmes, in all his finery."

"Oh, yes," Reinette laughed. "Where did he get that ugly trench coat and that top hat? Not to mention those very strange sunglasses. They looked like some silly spectacles that Elton John might wear."

"That's right!" Estelle exclaimed as her mind surged, and the events once again became clear. "The hat and coat belonged to your grandfather. And I think he may have found the sunglasses in the toy box. But I don't know where the magnifying glass came from. He must have brought it with him."

"Oh, yes, I forgot about the magnifying glass." For a moment, Reinette seemed deep in thought. "Uncle Eli," she murmured, perhaps not realising that she was speaking out loud. "The Pied

Piper of Manhattan." Reinette sighed as she walked through the events of that day in her mind. Yes, as it turned out, the day had been better than even she could have predicted. "I only went on that outing because Uncle Eli said he would buy the tickets to a concert that I wanted to attend. And he promised me that he wouldn't do his duck walk in public."

"And you believed him?" Estelle squeaked, her voice breaking under the pressure of her laughter. "I knew that he would do it. He is such a comedian. You always get caught out because you always take him at his word." She felt content as she shared this special time with her daughter. She studied Reinette's face for some moments; of course, not wanting to be conspicuous in what she was doing. But she wanted to savour the moment and make sure that she had taken in everything about her. Perhaps if she worked hard enough, she wouldn't forget, was her hopeful reasoning. Within their close relationship, Estelle was relaxed and happy.

"Maybe I thought he wouldn't do it if I asked him not to," Reinette suggested. "Do you remember walking from the train to the museum? He duck-walked all the way, stopping at every shop to examine the things in the window with his magnifying glass."

"Yes, I do. He actually stopped traffic in the middle of Manhattan," said Estelle. "People began to follow him, spellbound by his antics, curious to know what he was looking at through his magnifying glass. And as I remember, you walked about two feet behind us, telling anyone who would listen that you were not related to that crazy guy up ahead."

"They were happy times," Reinette remarked. "And it makes me so happy that you can still remember." She took her mother's hands in hers and squeezed them. "I don't want to lose today," she whispered, her voice breaking as her emotions wavered, and the tears began to form in her eyes.

"Nothing is truly lost, Reinette," Estelle assured her. "Eventually, I may not be able to function as I do today, and it may appear that everything of me is gone. Don't you believe it. You, the family, my memories and everything that I am will continue. They will just be tucked away, hidden in the deepest parts of my heart. The body may die, but the spirit lives on." She gently tapped the Bible, drawing Reinette's attention to its importance. "You will find everything you need in here." Tenderly, she drew Reinette to her, and they spent quite some moments in a tender embrace. Neither spoke. Each knew where the other was in their thoughts.

Reinette was the middle child of five, where there were three boys and two girls. The family was originally from the outskirts of Minnesota, but they had moved to New York when Reinette was five years old. They had settled happily there, and Estelle's husband Gary became a successful trial lawyer in a large firm. For many years, their lives were more than comfortable. Gary was doing the job that he absolutely loved. It seemed that everyone was benefiting. Yet one of the family members was struggling. Reinette's brother, Franklin, could not settle in their new surroundings and became very depressed and morose. Reinette had many memories of seeing her mother weep as she read that Bible and plead with God to tell her what she should do to help her son. At the time, no one knew that he was bipolar, and that he needed more help than his family members could provide. So, the tension in the house was great, and everyone was on edge.

Yes, it was true that the pressure of dealing with Franklin's problems had taken a toll on the family dynamics, and Estelle and Gary began to argue about the best way to deal with the situation. He felt that she was pandering too much to the young man. In one of their worst clashes, he told her that if the boy didn't get a job and start pulling his weight, he should leave the house. She just wanted to keep Franklin at home for the present. She felt that with understanding and a soft touch, she could help him to work through his problems. This did not sit well with Gary. From then on, he began to spend more time at the office.

So, Gary came home less and less, choosing to stay at cheap hotels. He also began to drink heavily, starting early in the day. Estelle worried constantly about his health and welfare. She tried to persuade him to get some help. But all her words were in vain, for he wasn't interested. He totally ignored her pleas to let her help him. Frustrated with his behaviour, she gave him an ultimatum. Either he sought help, or he moved out of the house for good. But Gary didn't like getting ordered around by a mere woman. So, he told her to get a life, that it was his house and he would come and go as he pleased. And he did. He and Estelle now lived separate lives.

Then, one day, Gary was hit by a car and killed. He had been on his way to an important meeting and was somewhat distracted. The city streets seemed to be busier than usual that day. Cars, vans, trucks and busses were backed up, each vying for their own unique place in the bulging metropolis to do their business. No one noticed the unkempt little man who, was trying to cross the street in a hurry. He looked so small and somewhat out of place in his crumpled grey suit, red bow tie and black shoes. As he lay lifeless on the cold bitumen street, to some, he was just an old tramp who had no value, and they walked around him, continuing on their hurried way. Others stepped over him, disinterested in who he might be or how he got there. Then there were those who came just to see what all the fuss was about. To them he was a curiosity in the event that they could have a good gossip about with their friends.

So, what about Gary? What was his story? Yes, he had been in a hurry, as he was late for a court hearing. And yes, he could have taken more care if he had thought about it, but his mind was centred on the upsetting way that the case turned out. The client had been found guilty, and today would be the punishment phase. This morning, his task would be to argue why his client should not receive a death sentence. Therefore, several sets of factors had converged to bring about Gary's demise, and the outcome was devastating for everyone. Ambulance and police were quickly on the scene, but nothing could be done. Gary was gone, and someone would have to break the tragic news to the family.

Every bad thing seemed to come against the family all at once. What would Estelle do? It surprised Reinette that, within a couple of months, her mother was up and running again, positively looking towards the future. Still a very beautiful woman, Estelle applied for the position as a television news presenter at a local station and was successful. She worked there for the next fifteen years. It was at this time that she began to notice that her short-term memory wasn't so sharp. She tried to ignore it, but after a while, she knew that her life must change. Reinette lived nearby and became her visiting caregiver. At first, it was easy. Estelle volunteered at a local thrift shop. Reinette drove her there three days a week and then picked her up when her shift was finished. Estelle loved it. She made new friends, many in her own age group, and she became an integral part of a thriving community. Those with whom she worked knew her personal situation and tried to protect her as she helped out in the shop. They also visited her at home. At this stage, she could still cook and liked to bake cakes and biscuits for her friends. So, she gave little afternoon tea parties, making all her favourite goodies. This was a very enjoyable time in her life.

Reinette flipped through the old tattered pages and then closed the book. She didn't want to accept it as hers yet. Doing so would be like closing the final chapter in her family's history and she wasn't ready for that. Anyway, her mother could still read and so, she might still need it.

"You have so many memories tied up with this Bible," she said to her mother. "Perhaps you should take it with you. There are lots of little notes that will remind you of people, places and special things that have happened to you over the years. I want you to be able to know those things for as long as possible."

"No, no," Estelle quickly replied. "I want you to have it. You are the only one that I can truly trust to take care of it. The others don't understand the importance of it. My grandma gave it to my mom. So, it is a family heirloom. Yes, it is very special to me but I don't need it to remind me of the important things that have happened in my lifetime. They are already hidden deep in my heart. Although I may forget them in the short term, they will never truly be gone, because they will continue to live on through you and other family members."

Reinette nodded and sighed resignedly. Just then, Estelle got up and began wandering around the kitchen. In one of the cupboards, she found a colourful paper bag with handles. She picked it up and looked inside. An old receipt lay crumpled and unattended. She took it out, glanced at it briefly, and screwed it up. Then with such dexterity, she threw that piece of paper in the direction of the rubbish bin. Her aim was perfect, and the receipt landed in the bin.

"Wow!" Reinette exclaimed. "I'm impressed! That was a magnificent throw. I never knew that you were so accurate."

Estelle laughed and relaxed back into her chair.

"We used to have throwing competitions with crumpled pieces of paper when I worked at the television station," she informed Reinette. "I was the overall champion of the network."

I could see as Reinette took the Bible and put it in a safe, secret place in her house. She would have liked to display it in her living room, but she knew that if she did, it would disappear. Others in her family were not so honest. She knew this because about six months previously, Aunt Barbara, her mother's younger sister, who now lived in Australia, came to visit. She had never visited before, and honestly, she and Estelle were not on good terms at the time.

But Aunt Barbara was on a mission. Her quest was to acquire that Bible at any cost, even if she had to steal it. She felt that the old Bible should have been given to her in the first place. Therefore, she would only be taking what was rightfully hers to own. Anyway, she believed that since Estelle had that memory problem, she would not even notice that it was missing. This was her reasoning and plan. Fortunately, she had been very vocal in telling others in the family about what she was fixing to do. Another concerned family member rang Reinette to let her know. So, Reinette went to her mother's house and retrieved the Bible, taking good care of it, only returning it when Aunt Barbara was on her way home to Australia. The family didn't exactly say as much to Barbara, but hinted that Estelle may have lost it somewhere. Very sensitively, Reinette took great pains to remind Barbara that her poor sister had severe memory problems and that they were seriously concerned about her overall health. Estelle would soon need more care, and she suggested that other family members could each take their turn to help Estelle remain independent. Although very frustrated that she could not find the book, Barbara did not want to stay to help look after her sister. So, she gave up her mission and flew home two weeks later.

As I looked closer, I saw that the television in Reinette's living room was switched on, and news flashes of a serious virus spreading through certain areas of the world were being reported. It seemed an extremely severe situation, but at this point, it had not reached the USA. I was relieved to see that this new sickness may have been contained. Then there was a second newsflash. A shockwave, the realisation of truth rippled throughout my slender form as I then witnessed this new virus's transmission move into almost every nation in the world. There was panic-buying of food and household supplies as people were told to isolate themselves at home. Many businesses closed, some never to open again. Fear and anger raised their ugly heads, and close friends became foes when there was not enough to go around. Yes, humanity could be seen at its worst, driven by both need and greed.

I watched as Reinette, now a few months later, pulled out the old Bible from inside her wardrobe. Thinking it might be a good time to take a more in-depth look, she made herself comfortable in her favourite easy chair. She then opened the book to the first page. In bold letters, it said: "This Bible was presented to Sarah Jane Pemberton, by Reverend James Arthur Pemberton, dated January 26th 1831, being her 16th birthday."

Reinette hadn't heard that these people had been in her family, but if she looked further, perhaps there would be a clue. So, she turned the page. Here she found the marriages, births and deaths, a pointer to events of how the book may have been passed down through the family. Most of the people she had never heard of before. However, it was interesting for her to note that three children under four had suddenly died of unexplained illnesses. Then there was an eight-year-old boy who drowned, and a fourteen-year-old became very ill with influenza. The doctors were not able to save him. Sarah Jane married Mr Edgar Jonathan Edges, a soldier stationed at Fort Snelling. They had nine children, and it was her eight-year-old who had drowned in a river near her residence.

Reinette leafed through the many pages of the book. Perhaps there would be interesting little titbits of information about her family that would give her a glimpse into the past. Suddenly, the pages fell open at 1 Corinthians 13, and a piece of paper fell out. She picked it up off the floor and turned it over. The heading read: "Mama's Lemon Pie". The recipe was written by hand, and the paper had yellowed with time. Yet I could still see the date that it was written. It was June 21st 1850. I watched as Reinette studied it, taking in every bit of information that she could glean. There was more to this story that she wanted to know.

Just then, a woman appeared at my side. She was around fifty years old and wore clothes from the 1800s. She also was interested to see what was happening in my vision.

"So, that's where that recipe was!" she exclaimed. "I wanted to pass it to my third girl, Julia, but I couldn't find it. My mama taught me how to cook that lemon pie."

It was a special moment for her as she watched Reinette take such notice of everything about it.

"And that is my writing," she informed me with deep satisfaction and pride. Her joy in finding that piece of paper just burst out of her thankful heart, and she began to dance. Taking my hand, she drew me into her happiness, and I pirouetted around the library with her.

It was a beautiful experience for me. I had not danced since I met up with Joel in a previous dream. My heart beat a loud *Thank You* to God for again allowing me to have this incredible expression of delight. We sat down side by side on the floor so that we could chat. It may appear that this was an unusual place to sit, but I was quite comfortable just being able to relax in her company.

"Are you Sarah Jane?" I wanted to know.

"Oh, yes," she replied. "My daddy gave me this book." She took the Bible from me and hugged it to her chest. Then she lay it on her knees and looked inside. Her touch was tender and her gaze steadfast.

"Let's look at Psalm 23," she suggested. Then she turned there. "The Lord is my shepherd," she read. "Do you know what that means?"

"A shepherd takes care of sheep, so it must be that the Lord takes care of people in the same way," I replied, my answer a little unsure.

"True, but it is more than that. Sometimes we can glean insight from natural things around us. Consider Benny, the cat," she encouraged.

I smiled as his little face came to mind. He could be a scallywag at times, disrupting Miriam's gardening and bringing all kinds of unwanted creatures into the house. Yet, he gives so much joy to Miriam, and I don't think she would want to be without him now.

"To Benny, Miriam is not just his caregiver. If she were, he would just turn up for food and a place to sleep," Sarah Jane explained. "No, Benny has, in fact, abandoned himself to her care. Miriam is his person, family. There is nowhere else for him to be. In the same way, if you abandon yourself to the King's way that is written in his book, he will write those things in your heart and he will always be with you. He can be your person wherever you happen to be. He will be your wisdom in all situations, your wingman beside you in all your adventures, and your champion who will defend you when evil comes knocking at your door."

I nodded. It was a big truth to absorb, but I needed to know more.

"So, who is my person right now?"

Sarah Jane laughed. She seemed pleased that I had asked the question.

"You are trying to run your own life, Robbie. Until now, you have been your own person," she said. "So, how is that working out for you?"

"It didn't work out too well when I tried to stop that guy from stealing my purse," I grumbled. "He had the measure of me from the start."

"This is because the boy saw his opportunity and took advantage of your disability. So, there was little hope that any person in the vicinity of the park could have helped," she said, laying out the facts to me. "He even counted on Pete's disability to slow him down. He had figured out that Pete could not move fast enough to stop the robbery. However, these plans were formulated in only a couple of minutes. The boy was in great need and you became his source. It seemed that there was no one to help you, yet here you are. What do you think about that?"

"Yes, I am beginning to realise how blessed I am. It is true: The King is my shepherd. He knows me, and that's amazing!"

"Do you know where you are right now?" she enquired.

"I've heard about the heavenly place where God and Jesus live," I informed her. "And this place is as close to it in my mind as I can imagine. The King most reminds me of Jesus because he has all the marks of having been on that cross. So, I must be in Heaven."

Sarah Jane laughed as she tenderly stroked my arm. In that moment, she reminded me of Miriam in the way she embraces everything that I am without regard for my failings. So, I was perfectly relaxed in Sarah Jane's company. She then pointed to another verse in Psalm 23.

"Look at these words, Robbie," she exclaimed. "Perhaps they are talking about where you are right now." And she read the verse aloud. "Yea, though I walk through the valley of the shadow of death, I will fear no evil, for you are with me; Your rod and Your staff comfort me. Do these words speak to you, Robbie?"

"Shadows are where the sun isn't," I replied. "They can be anywhere. The shadow of death sounds scary, but wherever I have seen shadows, the sun is not far away. So, I just move to a different location. Perhaps it is the same with the shadow of death. With the King nearby, death has no power because all I have to do, is move over to where he is. While the King is my person, I am protected from evil. Is that right?"

"Excellent!" she sang and clapped her hands with approval. It was as though I was a two-year-old visiting a sweet shop, choosing my favourite lollipops. Yes, I loved her exuberance. However, I began to feel somewhat burdened. There was something I needed to know. But what was it? I turned to look at the books. They seemed to sparkle in the sunlight. Yet my gaze was drawn back towards the old Bible. I guessed there could be more to the story of Reinette and Estelle, and I needed to investigate further. Quickly I turned to ask Sarah Jane for her advice, but she was gone. So, I was alone again. Suddenly, in the distance, I could hear the delightful melodic sounds of a choir singing a hymn. Putting the Bible under my arm, I walked toward where I thought the music originated. I was determined to know more.

CHAPTER NINE

As I approached the music room, goosebumps went right through my body, and my muscles jumped and popped with delight. Even from some distance away, I could hear the beautiful melodic voices of the heavenly choir. Both the words and the music inspired me to sing and dance, joining in with their tribute to the King of all Kings. It was amazing. I found that all the words and the music seemed to emanate out of every part of my being. They were an extension of who I am, intrinsically infused into my soul, a gift from my Creator. Yet it was an unfamiliar sensation, something I hadn't experienced before. So, I wondered if I was mistaken. Was it really me that was openly verbalising the worshipful praises to Him? Or could someone else be singing close by and my ears perhaps deceiving me? After all, I had never been able to sing before. But no. It really was me. My own lips were moving, and that was definitely my voice breaking through the rainbows of sound. Even outside the music room, I was participating in this incredible concert. I was excited. Here was where I wanted to be. So, I opened the door and stepped inside.

"Hello, Miss Robbie," said the choirmaster. "We have been waiting for you. Look! We have made a place for you." And he gestured with his hands to where there were, in fact, two spaces available. This stirred my curious glands into action, and I was determined to know more. After all, both the available places were in the middle of the front row of the choir. So, there was no mistaking that more than one person belonged there.

"Hello," I acknowledged the choirmaster specifically. Then I turned to include them all, "You have such beautiful voices," I remarked. "I usually can't sing, but your voices have inspired me so much, giving me such joy that I wanted to sing and dance with you. Isn't that amazing?"

"Yes, yes, yes," they all exclaimed, clapping with great pleasure and happiness.

"I see you have two available spaces in your choir," I noted. "Are you expecting someone special to arrive?"

"Everyone who comes here can sing, Robbie," he said. "Even you. And you have a beautiful voice. Come and join us." And he extended his arm to encourage me to join with them. "Oh yes," he added. "That space is reserved for someone very special. He is the young man who stabbed you in the park. The King has given him a great gift of music, and with help, he will be a famous musician one day. But even to this point, his path in life has been fraught with danger. Life has not been easy for this young man. It is in your hands to show compassion. Also, he needs your understanding and forgiveness."

The heavenly choir sang in soft and soothing tones as they gathered around me to support and help me bear the scenes I was about to witness. Just then, a new scene opened up before me and I was an unseen witness at the birthday party of a seven-year-old boy. Somehow, I knew that the next few minutes were going to be tough. Yet, I could not look away.

So, I was at his birthday party. Many of his family had come together in celebration. One of his uncles had brought him a special birthday gift. It was a handmade guitar. With great care, the boy ran his hand over the instrument, observing everything about it. A warm sensation rippled through his entire body as he saw that his uncle had etched a name on the front, underneath the strings. This name couldn't be clearly seen from a distance, but looking closely, each letter of the word seemed to give him permission to smile broadly. CHOCCO, it read. This had been his family nickname for many years. For a few moments, he was able to put aside the anguish of his home life to concentrate on having an untroubled couple of hours with his wider family. Again, he ran his fingers over the polished wood and strings. Yes, he would treasure this present, and his spirit rose up within him, determining that he would learn to play.

At this time, he felt the stony stare of disapproval by his stepfather, and he shivered with fear. At that moment, his delight turned again to reticence. He gently and quietly put the guitar down on the table. Then he backed away. This was his favourite gift, but he dared not show it. Past experience had taught him that he must hide his happiness well; otherwise, he would not have that guitar very long. There was a moment when he and his stepfather locked eyes. And he didn't miss the sullen sneer which let him know that an evil look was following his every move. He must be more watchful from now on.

The sadness and hurt I saw in the eyes of this seven-year-old was heartbreaking. He wished that his mother had not stayed with this awful man all these years. He was caught in a whirlwind of other people's bad choices and behaviour. His mother loved him dearly, but she was a victim herself and felt helpless and unable to make things right for them both. The video of his life showed me how he had drifted from one disaster to another. When he was nine, his biological father died in a gang-related incident. Although his mother and father hadn't been together since he was a toddler, there was still a sense of relationship between them. Now and again, his father would turn up at one of the boy's rugby matches, disappearing before the game had finished. As a child, Chocco set his sights on becoming an All Black and dreamed about leading the New Zealand team to victory over Australia or even South Africa. In his imagination, he was the one that scored the most tries and received all the accolades.

Yet as he neared his teenage years, Chocco lost hope that anything good would ever come his way. He became despondent and sullen, communicating very little with anyone and spending more time away from the house. By day, he hid in dark corners, suspicious of anyone who gave him close attention. His survival depended upon what he could borrow or steal, yet returning on occasion to the house to make sure his mama was still alive. Then one day, he decided not to go home ever again. He just didn't think it was worth the hassle. As soon as he appeared in the doorway, his stepfather would be on his feet, walk over and begin pushing him around. Chocco knew he was now strong enough to beat the older man in a fist fight, but he thought it best for his mama's sake not to touch him. The consequences for her would be horrific. By now, she could not hide the bruises all over her face, arms and legs. There was no telling of what his stepfather might do to her if he was provoked.

Anyway, people of the streets had recently taken Chocco under their wing and were teaching him new ways to survive. Although he was still living rough, he felt more secure. Now he had friends he could rely on, and his food supply wasn't so difficult to come by. During this time, his mother did try to find him. The school truancy officer had come to inquire why Chocco wasn't attending classes this semester. She was embarrassed and felt that it was perhaps her fault that he had run away. If only she had the courage to stand up for him more, she mused. But her husband had warned her not to let the boy back into the house. He said that she would be sorry if he caught him there. She knew full well that life could become complicated if Chocco returned to live with them. So, she stopped her inquiries and waited to see if he came back on his own.

After his seventh birthday party and while the stepfather was out in his garage, Chocco's mother had taken the guitar, and wrapped it in a large towel. Then she and her son went into the laundry.

"We will put it in the hot water cupboard for safe keeping," she said, then warned him to choose his times well to practice. He knew exactly what she meant and nodded his agreement. Quickly and quietly, she put the guitar in the back of the cupboard, under some unused blankets, a place where her husband would not easily be able to find it. Years later, when he left home for the last time, he took that guitar from its hiding place and carried it with him constantly as he went from one place to another.

This was a great deal for me to take in. Wow! That poor little guy. I felt suffocated as the pictures of the little mite played in my head. Momentarily, I reflected back on the scene of Chocco as a three-year-old that I had witnessed while I was in the company of the two elderly gentlemen from Morgandy. Yes, I was appalled at what I had seen, yet also amazed at how a child so young had survived being thrown against the wall by a grown man. Then to continue to live with that treatment day after day, year after year. There had been no break, just constant fear in the knowledge that at any moment, peace and calm could turn to chaos and excruciating pain. Perhaps one day, there could even be a murder. This man that they lived with was very dangerous. My heart went out to that little boy and I wanted to scoop him up into my arms, hold him close, taking away all his pain and make everything all right. On the other hand, as far as the stepfather was concerned, I was so angry that I wanted to take hold of his head and pound it into the floor until he screamed for mercy. This was such an intense feeling that seemed to take me over. Suddenly, my breathing became laboured, and I felt physically drained. My body swaggered as though drunk. It was almost like I was back in my disabled body and I was afraid. No, no, no. Inwardly, I fought to take control to regain the freedom of ability I had before. But to no avail. I was fading fast. *What would happen now?* I wondered.

"Robbie, Robbie," someone was calling to me. His words sounded as though they were emerging from the crashing waves of a turbulent sea, thunderous and powerful. Then, as I began to fall to the ground, two strong arms reached out and caught me and immediately, my strength returned so I could stand, and I felt safe. I looked up, and there He was, my Saviour, the One who gives me life and strength. Yes, the great King, the ruler of this heavenly realm, was now holding me. As He came into view, the choir moved back and bowed in respectful homage, acknowledging who He was in song. "Robbie," He said again, almost a whisper this time. "Don't become what that man is," He advised. "His heart is full of uncontrollable anger and hate. Therefore, other people in his life are the recipients of his bad behaviour. He hurts everyone around him. Concentrate on the boy, Chocco. He has a soft and pliable heart. He desires to do what is right and good, but his heart is broken, and his spirit is crushed. We can work with that. As you have seen thus far, he has had a life of horrific pain at the hand of his stepfather. And also, as you have experienced, it is so difficult to watch. Yet if you only concentrate on his past and his pain, letting your angry thoughts take control, you will become weak and sickly. You will have no power. Revenge is an utterly destructive mechanism in your body and your soul. Put your energies into activities that work to build you up. Then you will be able to help others. You are strong and able, even within your disabilities."

"But my disability is gone now, and I don't want it back," I declared, nose in the air, determined and resolute. Looking into the eyes of compassion, I realised at that moment that His reply may not be what I would want to hear. But then, it didn't seem to matter. I was happy to simply be in His company and to have the opportunity to absorb some of His infinite wisdom.

"Your disability is nothing compared to who you are as a person, Robbie," he said. "In fact, everyone thinks they have a disability of some kind. Some hate the way their nose sticks out, or their mouth is crooked. You may not always recognise it, but it is there. Your disability is physical and comes with many challenges which others can see. Theirs are mental and emotional and cannot be easily noticed."

"Oh, I wouldn't have considered that to be a disability," I commented with a giggle. "In my estimation, that would be more of a pride thingy. I'd much rather have a strange-looking nose than Cerebral Palsy."

His eyes crinkled as His face lit up, and I could see that my comment amused Him. He sighed and put His arm around my shoulders.

"I'll keep that in mind," He laughed. Then He became somewhat serious, and I knew there was more that He wanted to discuss with me. "Your disability should be the least of your worries," He said. "There is so much more to you than that. My father and I have made you with unique abilities," He continued. "But there are also times you have used your disability as an excuse not to step out and take advantage of the opportunities We have made available to you."

Suddenly, I felt very uncomfortable. *Have I really done that?* I wondered. So, I decided to put the question to Him.

"When did I do that?" My inquiry sounded hollow and pathetic, as I knew it was probably true. "I don't remember that!" He looked back at me with a look of disbelief that exposed me as a naughty child, saying no to discipline and opportunities that would bring healing and true blessings to my life. At that moment, a memory opened up before me, and I watched myself as an eleven-year-old, refusing to learn to write with a pen. The opportunity had been given to me to learn new skills, and the physiotherapist believed that with some hard work, I could gain quite a bit of function in one hand. These particular exercises would have been good for my muscles, strengthening them, but I found them very painful and boring. So, I quickly gave up.

"You give up on things too easily, Robbie," He said. "You have desires, things that you would like to do. But as soon as things get tough, you stop even trying to do them. Deep within you, there is a passion that will lift you to the next level of your abilities. Unfortunately, you have suppressed that emotion, thinking you are not good enough to have those things you desire. This is not true, Robbie. It is a lie from the pit of hell to keep you bound up in the chains of your disability. You need to put aside those thoughts and believe in yourself. Bringing that passion inside of you and putting it to work will help you achieve your dreams.

I nodded, although I was still somewhat sceptical. Then my body again became weak, and I struggled to keep my mind and spirit on track.

"Understand this, Robbie," He said. Then He rendered His decree. "You are now in a battle for your life and future. The enemy thinks he has you in his grasp right now and will not let you go until he completely destroys you. He may well succeed, Robbie, because until now, you have most often buckled under his pressure. You haven't learned yet how to fight for what belongs to you. Do you want to live, Robbie? If so, you need to find the path in life that sets you on fire with desire. Then you must determine to travel that road. Turn neither to the left nor the right, but set your sights on the goal.

"There are good things in your future, Robbie. However, you can't have them if you sit at the side of the road as a spectator. Be a participator! Firstly though, you must decide who you believe. Is it

Me when I tell you that you are strong and able, even in the midst of dealing with your disability? Or is it your enemy who tells you constantly that you are weak and that there is no positive future for you because you are pathetic and useless? He wants to take all the good gains that you have made so far and scatter them to the wind."

"Who is my enemy?" I needed to know who I must not listen to or follow in the future. "Who is trying to destroy me and why?"

"You have read the story about Adam and Eve in the Bible," He began to explain. "Both were unique people. Created from the earth, We breathed Our own life into them. Then We placed them in a beautiful garden where they could develop and grow in every way."

I nodded. Yes, it was a fascinating story about two people who lived in a world where everything was provided in abundance. Their Creator gave them only one piece of advice. He said they could eat the fruit of every tree except the one in the middle of the garden. He warned them that they would surely die if they ate that fruit. So, they must leave that tree alone. Don't even touch it. And for a while, they were obedient. Then one day, a serpent appeared and told Eve that their Creator had lied to them. In his conversation, the tricky little reptile inferred that their Maker was holding back something important that they were entitled to have. He informed her that if she and her husband did eat the fruit, they would not die but become powerful and knowledgeable like God Himself, knowing all things. This appealed to Eve, so she reached up and picked the fruit. After taking a bite, she handed it to her husband. Without hesitation, he also ate the fruit. Interestingly, after the deed was done, the serpent was not heard from again. But as for Adam and Eve, although they gained power and knowledge to run their own lives, their close relationship with the Creator was broken, and they were banished from the garden.

"We don't have snakes in New Zealand," I informed the King. "So, it wouldn't affect me."

I could see His lips curl into a knowing smile, and He seemed amused.

"The danger was not in the appearance of the serpent," He replied. "But it was in the presence of the person who gave the reptile a voice. You know that voice, Robbie. He whispers in your ear all the time, and you listen. He creates fear, doubt and regret that constantly plagues you. Sometimes you think that you are going crazy. Perhaps you think all those negative thoughts and ideas just drop into your head from out of the clouds. Well, I'm letting you know today that they don't. Each thought is strategically placed in your mind to taunt you, to mess with your life. It was the same voice that Eve heard, telling her that she and Adam were not receiving everything they deserved. And because she stopped to listen, engaging in a conversation, he was able to convince her that they should turn their back on the Creator and take control of their own lives."

"Oh, I was under the impression that those thoughts were coming out of my memory, reminding me where I have failed in the past. But yes, they do have a negative affect on me."

"You are absolutely right," He said. "When you start listening to those negative statements about yourself and agree with them, you are giving them voice and permission to affect your life. Then your body becomes stiff and unbending. You can't do the same things you did only a short while ago, and you wonder why. New thoughts appear, telling you that your health is on the downturn and you could die. At this point, your confidence in yourself is very low."

"So, who is this enemy?" I quizzed him. "What is his name?"

"A long time ago, he was one of the most loved angels in Heaven," the King informed me. His voice held a hint of sadness and regret, and I sensed that He wasn't keen to go into detail. Yet He did want me to understand why those annoying influences tended to slow down my progress and caused me to feel unable to do even the simple things in life. "We miss the person that he was," He continued. "Yes, a beautiful spirit, adorned in the brightest colours and blessed with the greatest gifts of service. He was the chief of all the angels and we loved him. But pride and greed took over, as he sought to step into the shoes and replace his Creator. Very quickly, he amassed a following, taking one third of the angels with him. Under his leadership, they stood and opposed the highest authority in the universe. The Creator had no choice but to banish him from living in our home. Now he does all he can to destroy everything good that has been built on earth. Silently, he roams the dark places of the universe and looks for situations and people where he can infuse his influence. Deception is his biggest strength. He will implant a negative thought in your mind and wait for you to run with it. Then as you entertain that concept and all the feelings that go with it, he will add a little touch of bad memories, guilt and regret so that your confidence begins to wane."

Yes, I understood exactly what He was saying. I go through those battles every day.

"So, what should I do?"

"You have heard the saying, 'God don't make no junk.'"

I smiled to myself. Yes, I remembered that my Uncle Carl would tell me that all the time when I was growing up and finding life difficult. Carl was Edna's husband, a successful businessman in Auckland but he died quite suddenly of a heart attack. He and Edna didn't have children. So, when Carl passed away, Edna moved to our little town. Here, she could be closer to her favourite niece. And who is that? Me, of course. Suddenly, I recalled all the fabulous people who have stood with me on my life's journey, and I missed them. Each one has a special place in my heart. They have always loved me, no matter what, and encouraged me to venture into uncharted waters. They have supported me on the few occasions where I have taken a risk to go further and applauded me, even when I have not succeeded in my goals. Yes, I am truly blessed and happy.

"You will return to your life on earth, Robbie," said the King. "And you will be disabled with Cerebral Palsy as before. But as you remember your time here and study the words of wisdom from My ancient books, you will find strength to resist the temptation of listening to those negative voices. Look at me, Robbie," He commanded. "Listen only to My voice. I say that you are strong! I say that you are able! And if you take Me at my word, allowing Me to guide your thoughts and beliefs, you will become an outstanding beacon of hope for others." He put His arm around my shoulders and drew me close to Him. "But before you go back to your family and friends," He whispered. "I want you to experience something that will excite your heart. A lovely young lady called Judith will escort you."

Hardly a moment went by before a beautiful woman appeared. Her face glowed with delight at being with her King and Master. He had personally set her an important assignment. I could tell she was totally abandoned to His service and was happy and fulfilled. There was a spring in her step as she came to join us, an athlete with great ability. Her clothes were like those of a tennis player. And suddenly, so were mine. The choir all waved me goodbye, and Judith took my hand. I was off to my next adventure.

CHAPTER TEN

"I'm so happy to meet you, Robbie," said Judith. "What a beautiful day to spend with you. Let's sit over here by the river."

The warmth of her smile poured into me like liquid honey that flowed just like a river as it quenched the need of a thirsty city. Yes, I was eager to get to know her too. Around her neck hung a beautiful necklace, a unique piece of jewellery combining a gold chain and a finely hand-carved greenstone Koru. I could tell that this magnificent artwork had been a special gift from someone very close to her, her mother. It was an heirloom that had been passed down through the generations. She touched it several times, perhaps remembering her benefactor and making sure that it was still there. The Koru is a special Māori symbol, resembling a rolled-up silver fern leaf and is often designed specifically for the person to whom it is gifted. She also wore similar earrings, but they weren't a set with the Koru. We sat down and soon began to chat about things that interested us both.

Judith John had been a world champion tennis player in life. She, too, was a Kiwi, born in Wellington, New Zealand. However, to further her aspirations in the sport she loved, she and her family had moved to the USA. Living in the bustling metropolis of Manhattan, their days had become filled with learning new ways to commute and settling into a different routine. Also, there was a need to make important connections in the tennis world while working to implement long-term plans. Soon, she caught the eye of one of the nation's top tennis coaches, and they began to build her future in tennis. She had also won the heart of another up-and-coming player. After a four-year courtship, she and Rod became engaged. Yes, Judith was excited about the future. Everything was falling into place for her. She and Rod would move forward together in pursuit of championships worldwide in this wonderful sport. She now felt the greatest joy of distinction in triumph touch her life and permeate her whole being.

It is true that even at nineteen, Judith was taking the world by storm with her amazing gift. She had already won a Masters 1000 tournament and had gained a wildcard entry into the next USA Tennis Open. She was excited, as was her support team. Preparations were keeping her extremely busy, but she didn't mind. She was fully focused on her goal to go as far as possible at the USA Open and then to continue building her portfolio and entering other tournaments. Then one day, tragedy struck. It came like a bolt out of the blue, a dark cloud covering the sun and bringing winter's cold chill to every heart.

It was a Thursday afternoon. To everyone's dismay, Judith could not be located. It seemed that she had just disappeared off the face of the earth. This was such a mystery to all who knew her. Judith, a very social person, was always in touch, posting updates on social media. Her mother had tried to reach her by mobile phone but to no avail. So, she then rang the police and reported that she had last talked to Judith that morning at about 10.30am. It was after her workout at the gym. She said that her daughter let her know that she had decided to walk to a nearby shopping mall to look at clothing she needed for her honeymoon. But as her mother reported, she had never returned home.

The wait to see if she did get in touch was terrifying. Yet it had to be. Police must wait 24 hours, just in case she returned on her own. So, family and friends mounted their own private search. And because she was such a well-known figure, many in the community joined in. The local media also became involved. Investigative reporters followed the searchers, doing live broadcasts on both radio and television. This stirred many others to want to look for her. The next day, an official police inquiry began. Search and rescue dogs were used in all areas of the investigation, but no sign of her was found in the areas where they thought she might be. Two days later, her slain body was found in a wooded area a few miles away on the outskirts of the iconic village, Sleepy Hollow. She had been found by an elderly gentleman who always walked his dog in that area each day. Understandably, he was very distressed and had to be treated for shock by the medics. It had been a vicious attack. Judith showed signs of having been severely beaten with a blunt object and then, like me, had been stabbed. This was not a scene he would want to come across ever again. Later, he commented to a television reporter that it was a very sad ending to a life so bright and full of great promise. In a live television interview, the police made a statement, revealing that they believed she had been targeted and could not rule out the possibility that the perpetrator was known to her.

It surprised me to discover that Judith was a close friend of Reinette and her mother, Estelle. In fact, Estelle often joked, saying that she might as well adopt Judith into the family, as she and Julie, Reinette's younger sister, were like Siamese twins, joined at the hip. The two girls lived only two houses away and spent most of their spare time together. Judith had also been with the Evans family when Eli made his infamous impression of Sherlock Holmes as they walked to the Spy Museum. The two families were very close. So, when Judith went missing, everyone in the Evans family gathered around to help look for her, and they became the emotional and practical support for the family during that time.

The funeral was particularly sad. You know how things are with the media, always a finger in every pie, speculative opinions abound and shared. I remember that back in New Zealand, there were several live broadcasts on the national six o'clock television news. We all watched the coverage. A *Johnny on-the-spot* reporter relayed all the relevant gory details about the murder and investigation. Several extended family members and special friends had travelled from Auckland to attend and support the family, and other famous tennis players spoke about her exceptional talent as a sportswoman.

So the investigation began. Detectives worked tirelessly day after day to find the culprit. They used every investigative tool in their inventory to find answers. Yet every lead just fizzled out. Three years on, the killer was still not known. None of their tips panned out, which was also a source of great anxiety for everyone. For those closest to Judith, it was a heartache that simply wouldn't go away.

And for the police, it was a source of great aggravation. They had done all in their power to catch the person who did this terrible thing. Still, the decisive evidence wasn't there. So, eventually, they had to move on to other cases. But the detectives who had originally worked the case, never forgot her. Detective Harry Mann, the lead investigator when enquiries began, kept the file in the top drawer of his desk. He would take it out every now and then and look through it just one more time. He believed that if he could find that one elusive clue, he might discover who the culprit was, arrest him and bring some semblance of closure to the family. Yes, it was still a mystery unsolved.

"Let's go and play tennis," Judith suggested. "It'll be fun."

"I can't play," I squeaked. "I've never learned." But she wasn't listening to me. Grabbing my hand, she pulled me to my feet and began to run towards the tennis courts. The gentle breeze seemed to help us along. I imagined this was what it might be like to float on a cloud.

Judith gave me a tennis racquet and strolled around to the other side of the net. Then without warning, she threw the ball into the air, hit it hard, sending it quickly in my direction. In this place, my eyesight and physical reactions were exceptional. I could see the ball coming to me and instinctively, I knew what to do. It was fantastic. Yet there was a hesitation. Perhaps it stemmed from a past lingering fear of failure, of not being good enough to even try to give it a go. So the ball passed me by. I watched closely as it bounced in court, giving Judith the point. She certainly had a great eye and ability to put that ball exactly where she wanted, I mused. If I were going to be successful against her, I would need to put a lot more effort into my game. Wow! This was a surprise. Here I was playing a sport that had been impossible for me to participate in before. Tennis was absolutely my favourite game to watch. But I never, ever dreamed that I would actually have the chance to play myself. Wow! I was excited now.

"C'mon, Robbie," she encouraged. "Let's play." Then she threw the ball into the air and hit it hard with the racquet. At high speed, it came toward me, but this time I was ready. My eye was keenly set on that ball, and my muscles primed. No, I would not miss the mark this time. Suddenly, the air exploded with glorious peals of delighted laughter and clapping. It rippled through the universe, causing the sun to stand at attention and beam its rays into every corner. Yes, it seemed that the whole host of angels in heaven had been watching me, and they were excited to see me play. My heart rose to the occasion, releasing the joy of purpose and ability that had never been mine before. It was a fun experience, and I was having a great time.

"You know my story, don't you, Robbie?" said Judith as she lifted the ball above her head. Then she hit that ball hard. I saw it coming and moved quickly to where I could catch up with it easily. Jumping into the air, I hit that ball so hard, I thought it might pop. The joy of seeing it fly filled my whole being. *Wow! I love this place,* I whispered in my heart. I must stay forever. Suddenly, I was aware of Judith's gaze. She was awaiting my reply. Putting aside my reflective thoughts, I walked around to where she was on the other side of the net. She took my hand, walked over to a little bench, and we sat down. For some moments, I surveyed our surroundings. We were now in a small village outside an old-fashioned confectionery store. The paint was a little worn, and the sign was crooked. This village was nestled in a valley with warm green and gold colours, shaded by beautiful rolling hills in the distance behind and each side. I felt content here. My muscles were relaxed, giving me the freedom to be the best at anything I desired and the opportunity to create moments that would remain memories for all time. Yes, this was the place for me. I was sure that I would never have to leave. What Judith said next shocked me.

"When you return to your life, you will be successful," she assured me. "However, to uncover the identity of the person who took my life, you must follow the science, match it up with the evidence, and examine the life and movements of every suspect that has already been questioned in the investigation."

"But I only know what has been reported in the news. And I live so far away from where it happened. Anyway, I like it here best," was my reply.

Judith sat there for a few moments, silently considering what I had just said. Her smile told me that she did understand. Yes, this was the most beautiful place, glorious in its majestic atmosphere, a kingdom where the sovereign Lord knew, loved and spent time with each one of His people. His heart had captured theirs, and in His care, they flourished in every way. He also had a deep affection and faithfulness to even reach out to those with no time for Him. The contrast between my earthly life and here was huge. In my earthly life, I was frustrated by my limited abilities, struggling to do the most basic of things. Here I was healed and happy, joyfully engaging in my favourite sport. Nevertheless, Judith knew I was not yet ready to stay here permanently.

For most of my younger years, I felt held back from living a full life due to the difficulties that came with coping with a severe disability. Frustrated and depressed, I hid at home, not even trying to get out into the world and do more. Then I met Pete, and my life completely changed. Now I had a reason to get up in the morning. Opening his own life to me, Pete gave me hope, teaching me that even though I found day-to-day living quite distressing, I could learn to rise above my circumstances and work towards gaining happy and fulfilling outcomes. So, I set goals, and worked hard to make small improvements here and there. Over time I have come to respect who I am and to put extra effort into extending my abilities so that I can move on to the next stage of my life. It had been a long, hard haul, but now I was beginning to see some good fruit for all my efforts. Yes, I was very proud of myself for taking the steps that would turn my life around for the better. Day by day, my confidence grew. This is the life for me, I determined. Finally, I had broken through that barrier of discontentment, and I felt my own inner strength begin to grow. Over time, those around me also began to see the change and treat me differently. No longer was I perceived as unable to do many things, but as someone who wanted to try everything. But now, I was in this miraculous place, I was free from the difficulties of living with Cerebral Palsy. There were no physical restrictions here. Also, in this place, I had the ability to do many of the things that I had never had the opportunity to do before. I could speak normally, I could walk without falling over and best of all, I could play tennis. This alone filled my heart with unspeakable joy. Why would I want to return to my other life? The mere memory of even one of my former struggles brought a chill to my heart.

"You may think that you are ready to settle here and have your happily-ever-after life," Judith laughed. "But I don't know if the Kingdom is ready for you yet. There is a lot more for you to learn and experience in your other life. You need to go back."

As she spoke, I was reminded of my conversation with the King. And as I did so, I again felt healing and strength pour into me. I could feel my physical body respond and rise with excitement. It was strange because I did not need a tangible body in this place. Although I was complete in every way, no longer limited by the effects of Cerebral Palsy, only my spirit was here. My body was resting in a hospital bed, somewhere back on earth.

"Tell me who the killer is," I said to Judith with a sigh. Momentarily, I felt somewhat sad, and my eyes were downcast. Yet I knew that I must return to my other life for now. So, I put my shoulders back, lifted my head and stood tall. "Okay. Just let me know who he is, and I'll see that he is brought to justice for you."

"No," she replied with a giggle. "I'm not going to tell you that. You are quite capable of doing that yourself. And it doesn't matter where you are in the world. You will solve the mystery if you look in the right places and talk to the right people. You will know what to do at the right time. Oh, I see that someone is waiting for you." And she pointed into the distance.

I was immediately captured by the radiance of His great love for me. Yes, I could see it now. Quickly, I ran to Him. With arms wide open, He received me and pulled me close. For some moments, we stood there while angel beings popped in and out, dancing and clapping. I could see their happiness and appreciated their heartfelt welcome. He took my hand, and we went walking.

"So, you are enjoying your time here in our Kingdom?" He asked. "Pretty nice, eh?" His eyes smiled as He took time to examine everything that made Him happy. Nearby, a picturesque waterfall of blue and white sparkling drops of liquid life-force gave nourishment to the lush foliage of the mountain ranges. The sun reached down to each plant with alluring assurances of moments as an extra special blessing for the Creator. I could tell that He knew even the tiniest part of everything in this place intimately.

"Yes, I love it here," I said. My reply was tinged with a note of sadness and disappointment. "But I understand why you want me to go back."

With tenderness, He reached out again and His arms enveloped me and I relaxed into His care. His life poured into me. It was unstoppable, unfathomable, unquenchable.

"I have loved you all your life," He disclosed. "Before you were born, I chose you." His face creased, displaying little smiley lines as He remembered things I didn't yet know. But He would reveal snapshots of how He had been an integral part of my story all along. "Then I put you into the arms of my Father God. We discussed how difficult your life would be. Yet we were very confident that you would overcome every obstacle. But Robbie, your physical body is just your earthly overcoat. Who you are inside is the real you. As our special creation, we have equipped you with gifts of tenacity and strength to rise above your physical disabilities and a great passion for others, especially those in situations significantly worse than yours. So, we know that we can trust you to go that extra distance for them. You may think that nobody notices. We see it all, and it makes us happy.

"Wow," I gasped. "Are you sure that you are talking about me? It doesn't sound like the me that I know."

He threw His head back and laughed heartily.

"Oh, you are so funny, Robbie. I do enjoy our times together. Yes, I am definitely talking about you. Believe it, Robbie. You are strong. You are able, and you are smarter than you think. So, we want you to go back to your other life and do great things that will benefit others. Give them an ounce of your inner treasure, the special gifts that have been hidden deep all these years, and you will receive a ten-ton truckload of happiness in return. This is how our Kingdom works."

"What if I don't know how to do these things? Who shall I ask?"

"Don't worry," He replied cheerfully. "We have that all in hand. Before coming back to be with my Father, I told my disciples I would send them a special Comforter. He came and empowered them to do things they could not do before. He already knows you and wants to help. But He is a gentleman. He will give you a little nudge to show you which way to go, but He won't force His will upon you. If you need a friend to help you sort things out, He will be right by your side. And if you aren't sure that it is Him that you are hearing in your heart, just remember me and think back to the things we have talked about. You will soon begin to recognise His whispers of encouragement and guidance."

I nodded. Yes, I could anchor to that. He was so clear in His descriptions and instructions.

"What does the Comforter look like?" I wanted to know.

"What does the wind look like?"

"We can't actually see the wind because it is moving air," I replied. "But we can see and feel its effects. I like it when there is a breeze on a hot sunny day."

"That's right," said the King. "Having the Comforter as your friend is like experiencing a gentle puff of wind, a kiss on your cheek. Yet He is in your heart, an awareness that you are not alone, a go-to person who will advise you about how to do life and proceed to the next stage of your quest."

Suddenly He was gone, and my reality was changed. Opening my eyes, I surveyed my surroundings. I was now in a hospital ward. The pale green walls looked grey compared with the crisp white bed sheets that covered me. Brilliant shades of sunlight streamed in through the windows, and I could tell that we were several storeys above ground level. The cars and people below seemed small and far away. Life was continuing as usual outside my window. To my left, Dad sat in an easy chair, happily asleep, snoring loudly. He looked so relaxed and peaceful that, for a few moments, I didn't want to disturb him. But no. He wasn't going to get away with that. We had work to do, and there was no time for sleep or laziness. Strangely, I felt super energised and ready to go. Reaching over, I caught hold of his shirt sleeve and pulled hard.

"Dad," I called. "Wake up! We have work to do!"

He woke with a start, not knowing who was talking to him or what was happening. Quickly, he jumped up and looked all around.

"What?? What!!" he shrieked. I had given him a huge fright, and for a moment, he didn't seem to recognise where he was. I laughed, followed by having a coughing fit, which induced pain in my side. I had forgotten about my injuries. I tried to relax for some moments so the soreness would subside and I could breathe and talk freely.

"Still sleeping on the job, I see," was my next comment.

As he turned to look at me, he realised that I was awake and talking. The joy on his face truly sent a warm feeling right through me. Then he gave me his hurt look and put his nose in the air.

"That's enough of that, Madam," he scolded. "I've been up half the night consoling your mother. She's a wreck, you know. Anyway, it's great to see you back in the land of the living. How do you feel?"

"A bit sore. Anyway, enough about that. I need to talk to Mike and Jeff. Very important that I have a chat to them."

"The police are still looking for the guy that stabbed you," he informed me.

"Chocco?" I inquired without thinking. "Oh, don't worry about him. He'll come in on his own."

"How do you know about that?" Dad's eyes widened in shock.

"He's had a miserable life, Dad." Just remembering what I had learned brought tears to my eyes. The movie of the wee guy being hurled against the wall played in my mind. "The way his stepfather treated him and his mother was appalling. You have no idea."

"Well, how do *you* know?" Dad was perplexed. He pulled his chair closer and sat down so that he could hear more.

"Long story," I said. "I'll tell you all about it later. I need to talk to Mike about Judith John."

"Judith John? Do you mean the tennis player who was murdered? Why do you need to talk to Mike about her?"

"She's very nice," I informed him. "And she wants me to help find the person who killed her."

"Did she tell you who it was?

"No." And I laughed. "But we played tennis."

"Oh, well, that's nice," he commented with a wry grin. "So, while we are back here on earth, worried and thinking that you are dying, you are gallivanting away in some other realm or world, meeting new people and playing tennis. How could you?? I'm crushed!!"

"In Heaven, there is no email service."

"I'll try to explain that to your mother."

CHAPTER ELEVEN

Soon, almost everyone I knew became aware that I was awake. There seemed to be an endless stream of nurses and doctors keen to check on me. In hospital, nothing is sacred. They peered and prodded me everywhere on my body. The staff were astonished that my mind was clear and I was already giving orders. A medical technician came to take my blood, a regular occurrence in hospitals. Pulling the blankets up to my neck, I announced that my blood was too pure for their common tests and that I would call him when I was ready. The young man didn't know what to do, so he retraced his steps and left to seek advice.

Then came Mum and Pete. They fussed around me for maybe an hour, wanting to know if I had pain, how they could make me more comfortable, and if I needed anything to drink. Dad hadn't yet disclosed anything of our conversation about Chocco and Judith. I was pleased about that. Perhaps he sensed that I needed some time to relax and heal before dealing with all the awkward questions that Mom would throw at me. Anyway, I was pleased to see them. Pete looked tired and drawn. It appeared to me that he hadn't been sleeping well. Also, his clothes were crumpled. He looked as though he had been sleeping in them. I would need to have a serious talk with him when we were alone. Mom was very much quieter than I had ever seen her before. Although she is serious by nature, she is still quite outgoing and likes to involve herself in any social event. But now, she seemed somewhat withdrawn. It was very unlike her. I wondered if the events that had happened to Angela and I had taken a larger toll on her than she was admitting. Dad and I would discuss it in the coming days.

Dad had been away from my room for about fifteen minutes, when he appeared in the doorway. He had two people with him, a woman in her late thirties and a teenage boy. Quietly, Dad walked over to Mom and Pete and asked them if they would mind leaving the room for a short time. He said that these people needed to have a private conversation with me. I could see that Mom was not happy, but Dad assured her that he would explain things outside.

"Oh, Mike has arrived," said Dad. "He will be fascinated when I tell him about your dream."

"It wasn't a dream," I informed him. "If it were, I wouldn't know the facts I told you about earlier."

"A thousand pardons, Your Highness. I will tell him about your TRIP." And he bowed low to the floor.

"And tell him that he needs to get in touch with Detective Harry Mann in New York. He is in charge of Judith's case."

"Harry Mann, okay." He seemed a little distracted. "Anything else?"

"Oh yes. I'm starving! Tell Cookie that I need some of his good cooking. You can't trust hospital food."

He was laughing now. Yet there was still a seriousness in his manner. Quietly, he led the two people in and then stepped back.

"This is Jo Anne and her son, Chocco."

My mind jumped to attention, and I looked closer. Yes, that was definitely him. Fresh were the memories of his life review, and again I felt the heaviness of grief come upon me, knowing the things that had as good as ruined his life. He would have no pleasant recollections of his childhood. His mother looked stressed and afraid, probably thinking that we hated them. For the moment, only Dad and I knew who they were. Chocco would have to face the consequences very soon. However, the fact that he was here today pleased me. It showed me that what he had done, affected him enough that he would talk to his mama. Jo Anne moved closer so that she could speak to me. She did appear to be a little nervous but resolute.

"Hello, Robbie," she said. "Thank you so much for letting us come in to see you. I'm so glad to see that you are awake and doing well."

I nodded. There were many things that I wanted to ask her. Yet, I didn't think it was quite the right time. So, I waited to see what happened next.

"She's usually not this quiet," said Dad. "At home, I can't shut her up." His upbeat manner defused the tension in the room and Jo Anne and Chocco relaxed. When Chocco came into the room, his shoulders were hunched; he kept his head down. His mother took his hand to show her support and give him courage. Now that there was a better atmosphere in the room, everyone relaxed. And this was where Dad became serious. "Robbie says you have had a difficult time in the past few years. While unconscious, she went to a special place, where she learned about how much pain you went through with your partner."

Jo Anne's head bent forward, as she looked down at the floor. I could feel her embarrassment. The guilt weighed her down, reminding her of her failures, never giving her any peace. Perhaps if she had made different choices, her boy's life might have been better. Even now, she was still riding the old merry-go-round, putting up with the bad behaviour of her man, denying that the beatings even happened. She sometimes tried to devise plans that would provide a way out, but she was too afraid to take the ultimate steps to do what was needed. Now, here she was in a hospital room with total strangers, and they knew her innermost secrets. She felt awkward, exposed and afraid. Yet, everyone had been so respectful of her. It was amazing. Realising this, she believed that it would be okay to relax. And so, she did. She nodded, affirming that what Dad had said was correct, but she didn't elaborate.

"Chocco has been very upset and worried about you," she whispered. "He insisted that we come to see you before we go to the Police."

"Robbie said that you would come," said Dad. "She told me not to worry, that he would do what was right."

"Do you still have your guitar?" I enquired of Chocco.

"Yes," he replied. Quickly, he took off his backpack and showed me his precious possession. "I take it everywhere I go," he added.

"Play me a tune," I encouraged. "I want to hear you play."

He smiled and began to softly strum and pluck the chords that put together a melodic song. It was beautiful and sensitive. Yes, he did have a special gift from God. As he played, I was reminded of my journey to the glorious Kingdom of Heaven, where many amazing people live. Sounds drifted out into the hallway and through the building; many people appeared and hovered in the doorway. Everyone looked happy and contented. In the distance, my friend Mike, the policeman from Havenstream, spoke with Mom and Pete. Luckily, they didn't know who the two people sitting at my bedside were. Can you imagine the conversation, had they known? Also, Jo Anne and Chocco had no idea that the police were so close. It seemed a bizarre situation. I felt a little uncomfortable and stressed, thinking that any minute, someone would put two and two together and then all hell would break loose. Seeing my distress, Dad moved closer and rubbed my shoulder as he whispered to me.

"What's the problem, Sugar?"

Quickly, I looked over at Mike and then at Chocco.

"Oh," he said. "Don't worry. I'll sort it." He then went out, told Pete to come in and keep an eye on me, then pulled Mike aside so he could have a private chat with him. Meanwhile, Pete was giving me quizzical looks. I knew that he was eager to find out who Chocco might be. I took his hand and squeezed it. He relaxed and smiled. Even though he sensed that something significant was happening, he didn't ask any questions at that time.

Dad was away for about fifteen minutes. During that time, Chocco and his mother used the opportunity to speak to me about the robbery and stabbing. I could see that Chocco felt terrible about it and didn't know quite what to say. So, he relied on his mother to help him break the ice with me. He stopped playing his guitar and stood it against the wall. Then he leaned forward. Suddenly, he looked very small and fragile, pale and afraid. Yet, in the vulnerability of the moment, he also found the strength to try to make right the wrong he had done. I liked that.

"I am very sorry for what I did to you," he said. "I didn't mean to hurt you with the knife, just to steal your money. I know that was wrong of me, too. Yes, I should have asked. Mom told me that. But that is why I am here today. To tell you that I'm sorry."

As Chocco explained and apologised, I could see Pete's facial expressions begin to change. At first, it was shock, anxiety, and then concern for me. He didn't understand why Dad had let them in to see me. I understood his concern. Less than a year ago, he had found one of his best friends, Joel, murdered in his own home. Now he was here in the hospital, visiting me, who nearly died from a stabbing in the park, a crime he had witnessed. So, what should he do now? It was at this moment that Mike stepped through the door and walked over to the end of the bed. I must tell you that Mike's facial expressions are sometimes difficult to read. Therefore, I can't always gauge what he is thinking. He is very astute and can size up most situations, but he doesn't let on as to what he knows.

"Tell me your story," he said.

"Well, I'm back," was my reply. "And I was sent to solve a murder."

"Okay…" Mike rubbed his chin thoughtfully. "So, what do you want me to do with this young rascal?" He turned and looked directly at Chocco. "I've heard that he's been up to no good."

"He just needs a job, that's all," I informed him. "Get him a job!" And I laughed. He shook his head and sighed deeply.

"I'm a policeman, not a social worker!"

"So! When has that ever stopped you?" I challenged him. "My memory is still good. Remember Joel? And Timothy Sweeney?"

"Yes, I remember Timothy Sweeney." And he giggled as he remembered. "In fact, I saw him only yesterday. That was when I arrested him again and threw him in jail. He's still up to no good, even in a moon boot. I would've got you to deal with him, but you weren't available at the time. Now I'm told you were having a great time, elsewhere, being commissioned as a detective. What that's all about, I don't know."

"I'll explain about that later," I promised him. "Chocco is the one who needs help right now. So, treat him kindly, okay?"

"Okay, Boss." And he turned to Jo Anne. "Thank you for bringing the young fella to visit Robbie. It means a lot to her."

"Oh no, Chocco was insistent about coming to see Robbie." Jo Anne informed him. "He is devastated by what he has done, and he wanted to tell her how sorry he is."

I could see that Mike was quite impressed with this mother and son. As a policeman in a small town, he is more used to criminals who blame others or their circumstances for their continuing bad behaviour. For some moments, he stood there, perhaps considering his next move. Ordinarily, he would just go ahead and put the boy in handcuffs, then march him off to jail. So, what do you do with a criminal who takes the initiative and comes to apologise to his victim?

"I'll take good care of him, Boss," and he laughed and then turned to Jo Anne. "We'll just find a private place and have a chat."

Chocco put his guitar back into the bag and followed his mother and Mike out of the room. I relaxed as Dad and my mother walked in and sat down close to my bed. Suddenly, I felt happy to be back. Around me were the people that I loved most. The touch of Pete's hand on mine sent shards of joy right through me. I could sense his utmost relief and happiness that I had returned to him and that there was no lasting damage.

"You gave us quite a scare," said Mom. "I thought we had lost you forever."

"Samuel, Miriam and Eli are on their way," Dad informed me. "They have constantly been ringing to check on your progress."

"Oh, good," I chirped. "Eli is still here. He will be able to help us with the murder investigation. He could have some vital information to shed light on who the culprit might be. Anyway, I want to speak to him about his sister-in-law. I don't think that she should go to live in that nursing home in New York."

"Why not?" Mom wanted to know.

I was hesitant about replying. The things that I knew were quite shocking. We were still in March of 2019, and life was good. However, I knew life would change dramatically for everyone in every corner of the world within months.

"Well, dreadful things will be happening in the world soon. So, perhaps she should move to Texas, where she could be closer to Eli." Then thinking that I may have said too much, I added, "But what do I know?"

"It sounds like you know a great deal," commented Mom. "And it sounds as though she needs help. I can get our ladies to pray. What is her name?"

"Estelle," I let her know. "And her daughters are Reinette and Julie. There are others, but those are the main ones I know about."

"Okay, I'll get onto that," she assured me. "Oh, Aunt Edna and Uncle Edgar send their love."

"I hope you have someone watching Uncle Edgar while you are here," I warned. "I don't want to hear that he has burned the house down with his roll-your-own cigarettes. You know what he is like."

"Last time I saw him," said Dad. "He was sitting in Miriam's kitchen, sampling her cakes. There was an ashtray nearby, and all the windows were open wide. He looked happy." Glancing out into the hallway, he became distracted. "I'll be back in a minute," he assured me. Then he disappeared out the door. Mom and I chatted for a while as Pete looked on quietly, happy to see that I was returning to my usual self.

"Edna has a boyfriend," Mom confided in almost a whisper. Her cheeky smile reminded me of a naughty child's look when telling tales on a friend. Yes, gossiping is one of Mom's favourite pastimes. She and Edna can often be seen discussing the latest events and intriguing lives of neighbours while sampling a new coffee brew and homemade cake. "Can you imagine that!" she exclaimed, giggling all the while.

"Is he a toy boy?" I wanted to know. "Long hair, huge abs, able to lift a tractor and then do one hundred press-ups without taking a breath?" Mom and Pete exploded in laughter.

"Oh, you are naughty, Robbie." She could barely get the words out as she spluttered and choked on her giggles. Hearing the outbursts of laughter, Dad appeared in the doorway, followed by the rabbi, Miriam and Eli.

"We've come to join the party," he said. "We could hear you lot giggling from way down the hallway."

"Well, Mom has been telling me about Edna's new toy boy," I informed him. "So, is he a twenty-year-old fitness guru?"

Slowly, his lips turned upwards as just the thought of it tickled his fun glands. But he kept his composure, unlike the others.

"Nah," he responded. "More like ninety-nine not out, I'd say. White hair and a handlebar moustache. He's also more into country music; not a fan of the classics like us."

"Oh, wow," I murmured, my mind clicking over at a hundred miles an hour. I had heard stories about unsuspecting old ladies being conned by well-presented rogues who pretend to be rich when they are not. So, I thought I'd put the thought out there. "I hope he's got money then. We can't have Edna driven to the poor house by an old dude with a handlebar moustache. The fact that he doesn't like classical music is suspicious, for a start. I'll check him out later."

Suddenly, the room was filled with constant happy chatter and laughter. My visitors were all talking over each other. They sounded like bees hovering around a honey pot. So, it was difficult to know who to talk to first. There were dozens of questions. How was I feeling? Where had I been, and what had I seen? Then they wanted to know every detail, all in living colour. I couldn't keep up. But yes, I was glad to be back. My friends are so precious to me. I love being with them. Sometimes we have some oddball conversations, which brings us a lot of fun.

Later, Mike came to see me again. With him was another policeman whom I had never seen before. He introduced him as Sammy and let me know that although they had to arrest Chocco, he had been released into the custody of his uncle, who, unlike his stepfather, would treat him well. Mike also told me that he had been in touch with Harry Mann, the detective who was overseeing Judith's murder investigation in New York. I was surprised to hear that he had been given permission by his Head of Police to come to Auckland, bringing the file and evidence for me to peruse. *How amazing*, I thought.

"Yes," said Mike. "Harry said that he wanted to meet the victim who woke up from the dead and knew not only the suspect's name but also his life story. He wants this one for his memoirs."

CHAPTER TWELVE

I had been unconscious for twenty-four hours, but I woke up as bright as a button and ready to go. Doctors were amazed at how quickly I recovered. The knife missed all my major organs, though I believe, from what I have been told, that I lost a lot of blood. The staff said that I was their shining star, and many of them, including doctors, lined up a few days later to wish me well as I was released from their care.

As Dad wheeled me through the hospital doors and into the welcome fresh air, I gave thanks to my Lord, the King, for providing me with another opportunity to enjoy the wonders of this incredible planet. The sun rested tenderly upon my skin, not hot but snugly warm. It reminded me of the joy of Heaven, yet encouraged me to also treasure the good things I have discovered that make me happy here. I felt completely relaxed and ready to step out and *do*, not just try, but *do* great things.

On our way back to Havenstream, I eagerly took in the sights of the city of Auckland and beyond. Trying to drive in the horrific traffic of this great metropolis was sometimes very difficult for my poor father. I could feel his frustration as he navigated with a scramble of stop-starts, swerving this way and that, taking great care to avoid the possibility of disaster. Observing our surroundings, it appeared to me that everyone, both those in vehicles and pedestrians on their way somewhere important, wanted to be first in line and dominant on the street. So, they took desperate chances in their journeys that would put them in danger. Some wrong decisions could easily be the catalyst that might even end their lives. As an onlooker, I was fascinated, though somewhat nervous. I didn't want to become part of those sad statistics that we often see and hear on television news.

Momentarily, I looked firstly at Dad and then at Mom. They both seemed rather stressed. This was not a situation we were used to in our little town. *What should I do?* I wondered. Then I remembered my time with the King and what He had said to me. He had assured me that I had a friend nearby, the Comforter was His title, a "go-to" person on whom I could depend for advice. Silently, I prayed that we would be safe and that He would guide us safely through the traffic in this chaos of bad behaviour.

Just then, a car cut right in front of us. Fear gripped me as I closed my eyes and held my breath, waiting for the impending collision. As the other car had cut across our front bumper, there should have been a terrible accident. But nothing happened. Quickly, I opened my eyes and looked around. *Where was that car?* I wondered. For some moments, I could not find it. It had just disappeared. *That's weird*, I said to myself. I knew that it was an old Ford Falcon, red with a white stripe along the side. Where could it be? I am neither crazy nor blind. I had seen that car right there, and in my mind, I pointed to where I had seen it last. So, I looked harder and then I saw it. That stupid car was up ahead, in the next lane, weaving dangerously in and out of traffic. *We should stay back,* I decided in my mind. Dad was an excellent driver and didn't need instructions on what to do. So, I remained silent for the present.

Once we left the great hubbub of this metropolis behind, the houses of the suburbs also began to dwindle off, and the fresh, green farmland became our scenery. The naturally rolling hills and paddocks were refreshing to behold. The tension subsided, and everyone now appeared happy and relaxed. Dad heaved a sigh of relief and focused more on enjoying the drive. Mom rested back in her seat, closed her eyes and retired into her dream mode. So, it was safe for me to speak to Dad.

"Who's running our garage while you are away?" I wanted to know. Dad is a motor mechanic and has his own business in town. My brother Steven works part-time for Dad and often stands in for him when he is away or needs an extra pair of hands. I am very proud of my brother. He has worked hard to become skilled in fixing motors, just like Dad. But Steven is his own man. He is also a farmer. He and Jan love the country lifestyle, running a sustainable dairy herd of 300 cows and caring for other animals they have collected along the way. They also have four-year-old twin boys called Josh and Caleb. Thinking about them makes me smile. Now, it may appear to some that the boys have a speech impediment because they call me Auntie Wobbly. But no. They are articulate and intelligent. They gave me this name when they were toddlers and first learning to say my name; it has never changed. Steve, who has the same warped sense of humour as mine, thought it was so cute that he never corrected them, and now he calls me that too. So, Auntie Wobbly is who I am to them, and I don't mind.

"Steve is running the garage at the moment," Dad replied. "His friend Jason is helping out with the milking and farm work. But Steve told me that he's planning to employ Jason permanently. He wants to make some major improvements on the farm to extend its capabilities." Then he smiled to himself. "The twins have been telling me that they are coming to see their Auntie Wobbly," he said. "They have been drawing lots of pictures for you."

"I'll need to put aside a whole day then," I laughed.

"Yes, you are going to be busy," commented Mom. "The boys will be there when we get home. So, get your thinking cap on. You'll be enjoying their company all afternoon. Then Harry Mann arrives tomorrow from the USA, and you'll be working with him to solve that murder."

"He will be staying with us," said Dad laughing. "I don't think he could cope with Mike's way of life. From what I have been told, there is nothing in Mike's fridge."

"Yeah," I agreed. "Why cook for yourself when your favourite restaurant is just down the street? While Mike's around, Cookie's business is thriving."

The rest of the ride home was refreshing and pleasant, and the house smelled wonderful compared to the hospital ward. Oh, the nursing staff certainly tried to make us all as comfortable and relaxed as possible, but it just wasn't the same. Coming back into my home, I had that old familiar feeling, bringing joy, a knowing that I was back in my rightful place. Wheeling into my bedroom, I checked that everything was in place. The sun shone through the open windows, and I breathed in the splendid fresh air that came from God's amazing heavens. Next thing, a little furry head appeared through the window. He crept in quite slowly, measuring every step. Seeing that it was me in the room, not Mom, he jumped eagerly onto the bed and waited to be offered a treat.

"Hello, Bennyboy," I said. "How are you today?" Benny purred loudly and came and rubbed his head against my hand. He looked pleased to see me, and I knew he hadn't forgotten that I was overly generous with his treats. So, I went to the drawer to retrieve them. Benny sat expectantly on the bed. If there is one thing that I can say about Benny, it is that he is a gentleman. He waits until he is told that he can have them. I put a tissue down to protect the bed and placed a few treats in front of him. "You are a good boy, Benny," I assured him. "Only good boys are allowed treats." He looked up at me as if he understood every word, then tucked into his food. Mom disapproves of what I do with Benny and his treats, but I don't care. He is a sweet boy, and I like to reward him.

A few minutes later, a car pulled into our driveway and soon, I could hear a myriad of voices and excited chatter coming from the kitchen. I realised that it would be Jan and the twins. It wasn't long before I heard the hurried pitter-patter of little feet coming my way. They ran in to greet me, chattering loudly over each other as they came.

"Auntie Wobbly!" they called excitedly, "Auntie Wobbly, we drew pictures for you. Look!" And they dumped a pile of half-screwed-up papers on my bed. By now, Benny was long gone. As soon as he heard their little running feet, he took off out the window to safety. The boys were just too boisterous for him to cope with safely.

"Have you got a cast?" Josh wanted to know, and they both peered closely to see if I had any extra pieces on my body that would resemble something they could examine. "My friend Rewi had a cast when he broke his leg. He showed me, and I drew a Ford car on it. I like Ford cars."

"Rewi is my friend too, and I saw his cast. I drew a train, Auntie Wobbly. Mrs Simons liked my train. You should have a cast."

"Yes, how come you haven't got a cast, Auntie Wobbly?" Josh continued to interrogate me. "You should have a cast, and we would draw pictures on it for you." They were so focused on finding my cast that they almost fell off the bed trying to examine me. I was trying not to laugh, but it was difficult.

"I wasn't allowed to bring my cast home," I informed them. "Someone else needed it, so I had to leave it at the hospital."

"Ohhh." They seemed very disappointed and sat quietly contemplating what I had just said.

"But next time, I will bring it home," I assured them.

"Yes!" Suddenly, they were once again animated and talking over one another. "Tell them that you should bring it home because you need to wear it for three weeks and people need to draw pictures on it. Grandad can help you too."

Just then, Dad appeared at the door.

"Is everyone having fun?" he asked.

"Auntie Wobbly didn't wear her cast home," announced Josh.

"No, that's 'cause somebody else needed it," said Caleb.

"But she's going to wear it home next time," Josh added. "That's why we can't draw our pictures on it yet. I was going to draw a tiger."

"And me," yelled Caleb. "I can draw a tiger too."

"Ohhh," and Dad rolled his eyes. "A cast, eh? And pictures. Wow! Grandma would love to hear about that. And she has ice cream."

Within seconds, the boys were off the bed and gathering the pictures to show Grandma. Then they raced out the door, expectantly declaring the word ice cream as they went. Dad and I laughed, and he sat down on the bed.

"How is Angela?" I enquired.

"She's fine," he assured me. "At the moment, she is staying with Steve and Jan. It's a day-by-day process, but I think she is returning to her old self again. Having the twins around has helped in that they distract her from thinking about the bad stuff. She is more relaxed now and sometimes even laughs. You should hear what the boys say about her situation. It's hilarious."

"I can hardly wait to hear that," I laughed.

So, Dad got up and called the boys. Soon they came running, jumping on the bed and making themselves comfortable beside their grandad.

"I just knew you would need us, Grandad," said Josh as he licked the last remaining drips of ice cream on his spoon. "We can fix Auntie Wobbly's motor car. We can do it for you."

"Yes, we can," echoed Caleb. "But she'll have to get out so we can put it up on the hoist and see underneath. I could change the oil."

"Oh, you are such helpful boys," said Dad. "My best workers. We might do that tomorrow. But today, Auntie Wobbly wants to hear all about how you help Auntie Angela." He sat back, folded his arms and waited for their story.

"I help her," crescendoed Josh in his loudest voice. "I look for the bad man. He hides in the woodshed, but I've seen him and he runned from me, cos I a strong boy and I can catched him." His words became faster and faster the longer he spoke. I had to concentrate to understand every word.

"Me too!" Caleb yelled. He was not going to be outdone. "I gonna catched him, put him in handcuffs and take him to the jail." He nodded his head in constant agreement with himself. "I a strong boy, eh Grandad? I a very strongest boy."

Dad nodded affirmatively.

"Absolutely!!" he agreed. He was trying not to laugh and could hardly speak. I couldn't look at him for fear of dissolving into giggles.

"I the most strong boy, though," Josh interrupted in his loudest voice. And he turned to look at me for confirmation. "I will catched the bad man, an I will throw him in the jail!" As he spoke, he lifted both arms and lunged forward to demonstrate how he would do it. "You know I would, eh Aunty Wobbly? "

"Oh, yes," I agreed. "What helpful boys. Auntie Angela is fortunate to have you both to help her. You go get that bad man and tell him to leave Angela alone."

" I will. I will," they chimed as they ran around the room pretending to catch the bad man. It was like watching a pantomime.

Dad and I laughed, and soon, Dad joined in, chasing the boys around the room. They loved it. The noise of fun and laughter echoed throughout the house. Soon Mom and Jan appeared in the doorway. They chuckled as they watched Dad and the twins racing around the room, over the bed, up and down the hallway and back again. Yes, everyone was relaxed and happy, enjoying the entertainment. This had been the best homecoming ever. Realising I needed to rest, Mom and Jan decided to take the boys out for takeaways. The little rascals were delighted, and they dragged their Mom and Grandma to the car, squealing and giggling all the way. Four-year-olds talk so loud and fast. And when they believe that they are right, they talk louder and faster, and everyone must listen. So going out to eat was not an option for Mom and Jan. It was more of a command from the boys that this is what they must do.

Dad and I settled in the family room and decided to watch some television. I could tell that he was tired. His face was pale and drawn, and his body was slumped as he gave in to feelings of exhaustion. It seemed to me that the stress of the past few days was now catching up with him. I was concerned. Dad was not a young man anymore and needed to pace himself more these days. Soon he was asleep. I turned down the volume on the television so it wouldn't disturb him and went out into the back garden.

This was where I most often felt the nearness of my Creator. The remarkable wonders of nature, its vibrant colour, ambience and passion for receiving the life-giving nutrients that made the plants thrive, gave great credence to the belief that the earth and all its finery did not just evolve from a random ball of dust. No, the Master's handprint can be seen everywhere. There was quite a chill in the air this afternoon, a reminder that winter was not far into my future. Yet I felt exhilarated by the shivery touches. I would enjoy what this world had to offer in the here and now. I would reflect on my time in the heavenly place and mull over the things I had seen and heard. There was still a great deal for me to do in this life. I could not sit back and do nothing.

So, the King had sent me back to my life here on earth with a task or two and the ability to bring positive results. There was no time to waste. Yet, I would focus on remembering His smile for a few moments. There was so much to know about Him. As I rested in the memory of His face, I realised He knew everything about me: the good, the bad, the ugly and the beautiful. Yet He looked past all that and saw what I could be if I would only allow Him to help me. It was as though His whole essence had wrapped around me and transported me to a safe place of healing for my soul and spirit. I had never travelled this road before.

Suddenly, I felt a quick, sharp shock of wind like frozen water rush throughout my whole being, and I shivered uncontrollably. My muscles tightened and twisted until they hurt, a distraction that could veer me off course. Perhaps I should have gone back inside; my body was beginning to seize up with the chill. But I was in the presence of the Master Artist, surveying His creation. If there had been a different outcome and I had not come back, I would not have had this opportunity right now to appreciate His grand design and take part in all the exciting things this world has to offer me. I had come home to my family to fulfil my destiny and become everything I had been designed to be. Soon I would help to solve a cold-case murder. Now, that is what I call impressive. I could hardly wait.

CHAPTER THIRTEEN

Eli popped in to see me at about 4pm. He was anxious to ensure I was okay and find out about my trip to the Heavenly Kingdom. Apparently, Dad was quite worried about my mental state. So, he went to discuss it with the rabbi. It wasn't so much that he didn't believe me. All the facts that I had relayed to Dad were correct and had been verified. And this is why Detective Harry Mann was prepared to travel all this way from the USA so that I could help him with his investigation. But all this talk about a heavenly kingdom and meeting a murder victim was hard for Dad to absorb.

I was pleased that Eli had come to visit me. Now I would have a chance to talk about his sister-in-law, Estelle. Dad made a cuppa, and we all settled in for some good conversation.

"Your dad tells me that you went on quite an awesome trip while you were unconscious," said Eli. "I'd love to hear about that."

"Oh yes," I replied. " I went to the Heavenly Kingdom where the King lives. I saw your latest book! You know, the one you want me to help you with."

"No kidding!" he exclaimed. "What's it called?"

"I don't think I should tell you that," I responded. "You need to make that decision for yourself. You will know what to do when the time comes."

"Oh, okay." He became quiet and pensive. I seemed to have given him a great deal to think about. He sipped his coffee as he mulled over it all in his mind. He clearly needed to process everything he had heard before he felt confident to comment further. Dad also sat quietly, waiting to see what might come out next.

"Anyway," I continued. "We have more important matters to discuss."

"Have we?" And he laughed. "Tell me what you know."

"Your sister-in-law Estelle has the beginnings of dementia and is planning to move into a nursing facility in New York. Did you know that?"

"Oh yes," he divulged. "I'm going to sell her house for her and help her move. Estelle is such a sweet woman, kind and gentle," he said. His tone softened as he spoke of her, holding her in high esteem. "It is so sad to see that she has to deal with this dreaded disease. Sometimes I don't know what to do for the best."

"This is why you need me," I teased.

Suddenly, his eyes brightened, all his muscles seemed to relax, and he was again sporting that roguish smile that stirred my happy glands.

"Okay," he laughed. "Let's have it."

"Have you seen that old Bible that Estelle inherited from her mother? It has some quite interesting history written in its pages."

"Yes, she did show it to me," he disclosed. "She is very proud of it. I believe she has given it to Reinette for safe keeping."

"That's right," I agreed. "Estelle has a very pushy sister called Barbara who wanted to steal it. I wasn't impressed with her."

"Me neither," Eli said as he nodded his head and screwed up his nose. "She tried to enlist my help. I was not doing that!" His look revealed his determination. Estelle was his friend. He would certainly not help Barbara uplift that Bible from her sister's care.

"It was a gift to Sarah Jane Pemberton from her father, Reverend Arthur Pemberton, in 1831," I announced without even a thought of how it might sound to the two men. I was describing what Sarah Jane herself had told me. So, talking about it was fairly natural to me. Eli's eyebrows shot up with surprise, and I could tell he was taking a mental note to check it out later. I don't mind if people want to check out what I say for themselves. Often it's not because they think I'm making up these stories or that I'm just plain crazy. No, they just want to be able to support me better, and so they follow the trail of information that I've provided that will lead them back to the source.

"Sarah Jane was a fun lady," I revealed. "When you talk to Reinette, ask her about *Mama's Lemon Pie* recipe. Sarah Jane thought she had lost it, but to her amazement, it was tucked into one of the pages of the Bible."

"It sounds like you had a fabulous time while you were visiting Heaven, Robbie." Eli laughed as he considered my story. "Who else did you meet?"

"I'll get to that later," was my reply. "But we need to talk about Estelle's future. What you do now may be the difference between life and death for her."

"Wow!" exclaimed Dad. "That sounds ominous. What are you talking about?"

"Tell us what you know," said Eli. He says this a lot. It seems to be his favourite phrase. Well, at least it is a request, not a criticism.

"Moving her into a nursing home in New York might not be the wisest thing to do for her right now."

"Why not?" Both men looked at me quizzically.

"Within a year, life will drastically change for everyone everywhere," I informed them. "These events will happen so rapidly that you won't know what's hit you."

Suddenly, in my mind, I was back in the Heavenly Kingdom. There, I had been given just a tiny glimpse into future world events that would affect the way of life for all mankind. A new medical emergency, a pandemic, would sweep the world, turning lives upside down. People would be confined to their homes for months at a time. They would be forced to wear masks and unable to access certain businesses or travel to their favourite destinations. Food would be scarce as there wouldn't be enough workers to provide the stock. News reports would show empty shelves that should have toilet paper on them. People would fear that the shops would run out. So they would buy as much as they could and hoard it. I smiled to myself as I imagined houses full of toilet paper. Yet my heart also ached as I saw tragedy, despair, death and loss. "Don't let her move into a nursing home in New York," I recommended. "Move her to Texas."

"Why?" A little frown darkened Eli's face. "Can you explain it to us further, so we can better understand?"

"Sure," I replied. And in my mind, I recapped all the details of what I had seen concerning future events. However, I felt it best to reveal only the main points. "There is going to be a huge tragedy that will affect everyone." I tentatively disclosed. At this point, I wasn't sure how much I should tell them. Yet I sensed that for them to fully understand the seriousness of the situation, they must know at least some of the facts. "It will be a worldwide medical emergency, a pandemic. In the first few months, you will learn new terms such as *lockdown* and *new normal*. Central Government departments will tell you what you can and can't do. You will feel as though your life is not your own. Most at risk will be the elderly. I can't tell you too much more except to say that the stats will horrify you. This is why I'm advising you to move Estelle to Texas."

"Perhaps I should talk to Estelle." At first, Eli looked worried. But then he giggled. "She will probably think you are some crazy woman I've randomly met. Then she will tell me to get rid of those featherbrained ideas and refuse to move to Texas. So, I'll need to resort to using the big guns. I'll have to recount what you know about the history of the Bible. That will pique her interest. She will read that old Bible again from cover to cover to check it all out. And she will be totally captivated when I tell her that you are going to solve Judith's murder."

I laughed.

"I hope she doesn't throw a screwed-up piece of paper at you," I replied. "She is deadly accurate, and a missile like that could sting. She was the throwing champion when she worked at the television station."

As Eli pictured this in his mind, he laughed heartily. "I'm amazed at how much you know," he said. "Yes, Estelle's paper-throwing abilities are legendary in family circles. I had forgotten about that. But this pandemic that you are talking about sounds pretty bad. The jungle drums haven't started yet on that subject. Are you sure it will be as bad as that?"

"It could be something like Bird Flu or Mad Cow Disease," commented Dad. And he settled back into his chair, confident there was nothing to get excited about.

"Well, good luck with that," I warned. "So, when you are almost out of toilet paper, and there is none left at the supermarket, don't come running to me for help. I'm keeping all my stock."

"Miss Moneybags," laughed Dad, and he nodded towards me. "She'll be selling it to us at a profit, sending us to the poorhouse.

"Wow! Toilet paper, eh?" Eli's eyes crinkled as his laughter lines showed his amusement. "So, should we stock up immediately, or have I got time to get back home to talk to Shea?

"From what I saw," I replied. "I think it may happen early next year. But my advice is that you should begin now to stock up on certain items that don't have a use-by date. When I saw Estelle, it was around mid-January."

"I believe you," said Eli. Then he relaxed back in his seat so that we could enjoy our conversation. The atmosphere was now relaxed, and there was no longer any question about my mental health.

"The twins have been practising fixing your wheelchair," Dad told me. And then to Eli, he added, "they are four years old. Quite a handful."

Eli's eyes danced as he laughed.

"I have three kids," he revealed. "They are grown now, but I still remember when each one was that age. Going to the market was a real mission. They were into everything."

"My grandsons want to *mechanics* Robbie's wheelchair. So, they are practising on the kitchen chairs. My son Steven tells me they are very frustrated because the chairs don't have wheels and a motor, and he won't let them practice on the tractor. Apparently, they are trying to convince their parents that they need to come back tonight to visit. Be warned," he said to me. "You may have some little mischief visitors tomorrow."

"But Granddad will be nearby to rescue me if they become too much to handle," I suggested.

"No," Dad laughed. "I will be in Auckland, picking up Detective Harry Mann from the airport. I wonder how much baggage he will have if he is bringing all his murder files?"

"He may not have to bring the physical files," Eli suggested. "These days, they are able to access most things online. All he will need is a good, working computer or an iPhone."

"What a blessing," Dad laughed and heaved a sigh of relief. "I wasn't sure whether to take the car or the van."

"Would you like a passenger to keep you company tomorrow?" Eli wanted to know. "Harry and I met during the investigation, and we have kept in touch on and off. He's a very astute investigator. Nothing in his search for that killer would have been left undone."

"Sounds like he is a very caring guy," commented Dad. "Yes, I would appreciate some company on the trip. And you can introduce me to the detective. He'll be surprised to see you here, won't he? But on the other hand, having a fellow countryman here, will probably help him to relax."

"You will like him," Eli assured Dad. "Away from the office, he is very easygoing. We went golfing a couple of times. The only trouble is that he is on call in his job as a homicide detective and often has to leave at a moment's notice. So, it's hard for him to relax and enjoy himself.

"That's a shame." Dad was sympathetic. "So, he will enjoy the break. Maybe we can schedule some interesting events for him while he is here.

The two men chatted for a few minutes longer, and then Eli left. I watched him through the dining room window as he walked next door to Miriam's house. *Yes*, I thought, *he is a lovely man who'll be a good friend for Dad.*

The following morning, I awoke early. As the morning light became brighter, I began to sense that this day would be awesome. I felt excited, eager to see what this day might bring.

Passing by my doorway, Dad saw that I was awake and stopped to say good morning. He looked rested and focused.

"Do you think Eli would like to go fishing?" he enquired. "I was going to ask Harry if he would like to go out on the boat while he's here. But with Eli being religious, I don't know if he would like that kind of thing."

"Well, Jon Ward is a pastor, and he always goes with you," I laughed. "And from what I've seen and heard, he loves it."

"Yeah, but I've known Jon all his life," said Dad. "It's different when it's a long-time friend."

"Does he talk to you about God and Jesus?" I wanted to know.

"Oh yes," he replied. "We have some great in-depth conversations. I've learned many things from him about what the Bible says. And a lot of what he has explained to me makes sense." Then his lips turned up into a wicked smile. "But Jon and I haven't discussed your trip yet. I can't wait to hear his take on that."

"Me too." I laughed. "You know what he's like. He'll want to know every little detail. And all in living colour."

"I'll just send him your way for the full movie version," he informed me. "He won't be happy with my bits and pieces. And if I tell him while we are out on the boat, there'll be no time for fishing. He will badger me all day long to tell him the full story, exactly as you told it to me."

Looking briefly at his watch, he realised that he must hurry if they were going to be on time at the airport. I was looking forward to meeting the veteran detective. In the coming days, he and I would look at the evidence surrounding Judith's murder. Frankly, I did not know if I had it in me to solve a crime that serious. The investigators that do it every day are so perceptive and shrewd. They seemed to be able to gauge what really happened at the scene. I suppose this comes with time and the experience of doing the job for so many years. Yet solving this mystery was one of the reasons why I had been sent back to my life here on earth.

Jan and the twins arrived just after 9am. The two rascals ran through the house like a whirlwind, and the noise of little feet and voices was almost deafening. They were excited and curious. They were fast on their feet and into everything! It felt as though we needed an extra pair of eyes to make sure they stayed out of trouble

"You should get out of your car," Josh instructed me. "We need to put it up on the hoist, and so you need to get out."

"Auntie Wobbly can't get out of her car," Mom advised him. "She can't walk like you and Caleb.

"I walk good." Caleb announced in his loudest voice, and began marching around the kitchen. He looked like a little soldier on patrol. Not to be outdone, Josh did the same.

"I'm the best walker when we cross the road at the supermarket." Josh put his nose in the air as he stated it as fact. "Grandad said so." Then he turned to me and said, "My grandad went to Auckland. Where's your grandad?"

"My grandad is with God," I informed him. "Do you know where God lives? I bet you don't."

"Yes, yes," they both screeched excitedly. "I know, I know."

Mom tried to quiet the boys and settle them down.

"Shhh," she signalled. "Not so loud. Tell Auntie Wobbly where God lives. But speak quietly. We're not deaf… yet." And she laughed.

"God lives at Grandma's church," announced Josh.

"I've seen him," said Caleb. "He drinks juice with his sandwiches at lunch. I saw him."

"Yes, and he sits at a big table with his friends and eats his lunch," said Josh. "He wants me to have lunch with him one day." Then his eyes got big as he suddenly thought of something he might have forgotten. "I'm going to show him my favourite juice bottle."

Perhaps I should mention that in the Redeemer Church where Mom attends, there is a large picture on the wall of Jesus and his disciples eating the Last Supper. So, I figured that this was what he was referring to.

"Oh, really?" I encouraged. "Which favourite juice bottle is that?

"My Spider-Man," he eagerly offered. "God wants one like that too."

"He does not," Caleb countered. "He told me that he likes my green man. He told me that he wants to be green." And he nodded his agreement with his own thoughts as we all looked on with interest.

"Oh, wow! I didn't know that God wants to be green?" I replied. "I learn something new every day."

"But he can be blue," said Josh.

Just then, we heard Dad's car pull into the driveway. The boys went crazy with excitement, wanting to run outside to be with their grandad. Luckily, Mom and Jan were able to persuade them to wait inside. The three men appeared, and Mom got to work, making tea and coffee for them. I was introduced to Harry, and he pulled up a chair beside me.

"I'm looking forward to hearing your story," he said.

"Thank you very much for travelling all this way," was my reply. "I really appreciate that you believe me and are willing to take the time to work with me on this. I hope we can get some good answers to those all-important questions about Judith."

"Yes, it upsets me that I haven't been able to solve the mystery of who did those terrible things to her. I have her file in my desk drawer, and I take it out every once in a while so I can have a fresh look."

I nodded my understanding. Yes, I could see how it would frustrate the life out of him. He had seen firsthand all her terrible injuries that caused her life to be taken. Evidence had to be collected to determine what may have happened. He also had to deal with less than truthful people who purposely tried to hide their part in the crime to protect their own freedom. It was a mammoth task with a tremendous emotional toll. He looked exhausted but totally involved with everything around him. Just then, Josh sidled over to us, staring with wonder at Harry, waiting for an invitation into our conversation. The old detective smiled kindly at him and said hello.

"I'm going to fix Aunty Wobbly's car," Josh announced. "Can you lift her out, 'cause she can't walk like me and Caleb." Then he rocked from one foot to the other, waiting for Harry's reply.

"Wow? You can fix cars!" Harry exclaimed. "That is so clever. I never, ever could fix cars. Who taught you?"

"My grandad showed me how!" Suddenly, Josh was again very animated. The volume of his voice had risen about one hundred decibels, and he was so excited that he was tripping over every word. Not to be outdone, Caleb joined in, declaring that he could *mechanic* best. Again the noise was almost deafening, and I could hardly hear myself think. Just when I thought that my mind and ears could take no more, Dad came to the rescue.

"Ice cream," he announced. Suddenly, there was total silence, and all attention was on him. "But only people who sit down nicely and are quiet can have any ice cream."

Within seconds, the boys were sitting cross-legged on the floor in front of him, and not another word was uttered. I heaved a sigh of relief as Dad went to the freezer and brought out the tub of delicious dessert. They finished their ice cream, and then Jan informed them that they must go home now so that Grandad and Mr Harry could have a nap.

"I don't need a nap," they announced, almost in unison. "Cause I is a big boy. Grandad knows." Getting them out the door and in the car was a mission, but soon, they were gone. Silence is golden, believe me. I have so much respect for Jan. She is incredible in how she handles those boys. But for me, it was time to return to welcoming my new friend Harry and help him solve Judith's murder.

CHAPTER FOURTEEN

Starting work with Detective Harry was quite an eye-opener. He certainly had prepared well before coming on this trip. Bringing out a small suitcase, I noted that his equipment included a laptop computer, three portable hard drives and a large file with Judith's name on it. He took out a photograph of Judith and put it down in front of me.

"Tell me what you know about this young lady," he said.

I laughed.

"You sound just like Eli," I divulged. "He wants to know everything that I know all the time."

"Do you tell him?" Harry's eyes danced as he relaxed in my company. He looked a lot more rested today. Of course, his body would need a day or two more to recover from that long trip. But he was well on the way back to normal.

"No, I make him wait." I smiled to myself as I recalled times that I had held back on things Eli wanted to hear. Sometimes he wasn't as patient as he should have been, and I took advantage of that. I only give him the main points of what he needs to hear. Don't worry, though," I assured him. "I will tell you what I know about Judith." At that moment, I saw something that made me jump to attention. "This picture has something missing," I said.

"Oh really?" he shrieked. "Like what?"

"Where is her Koru?" I wanted to know.

"What's a Koru?" Little lines streaked his forehead as he struggled to understand what I was talking about.

"It's a special piece of Māori artwork from New Zealand. She wears it on a gold chain around her neck. It has been carved in greenstone in the form of an unfolding silver fern leaf," I explained.

"This particular piece was a family heirloom, given to her by her mother. She was wearing it when I met her in the heavenly place."

"Yes, Judith's mother did say something about that," he revealed. "But she was so distressed about losing her daughter that some of what she told me was garbled and didn't make sense to me."

"I will show you what a Koru looks like." And I opened my digital tablet and went to a page I knew of on the net. There were several styles of different artists' impressions of the Koru. I could see that he eagerly noted everything I showed him. "The word Koru means loop," I added. "It is a very sacred symbol, and she would not take it off except in extreme circumstances."

"She wasn't wearing any jewellery when she was found." His voice held a tinge of sadness as he reflected on what he had seen the day her body was discovered.

"Not even her earrings?" I wanted to know.

"Nothing," he emphasised. "Not even her engagement ring. We questioned her fiancé, Rod, about it, but he denied knowing where it might be. We even searched his bedroom at the family home. There was no sign of it. Actually, there was one thing that we all thought was rather strange." Harry gazed reflectively into space as he spoke. It seemed that he was trying to remember something important that he had long forgotten. "Rod's mother, Ms Hunter, tried to interfere with the search. She attempted to steer us in certain directions. I had to get an officer to escort her outside before we could make any headway. But in the end, we didn't get anything useful."

"Didn't you search the whole house?"

"No. The warrant was only for his bedroom, but we didn't exactly tell Ms Hunter that. I just waved it in front of her face at the door, and she let us in." He smiled as he remembered. "We didn't find anything that was suspicious in there. The room was clean. Yet she was acting very strangely. So, just to see what might happen, we gathered some screwed-up paper from the floor beside the bed and took it as possible evidence."

"Perhaps she fancied herself as a budding detective." I couldn't help but giggle to myself as I pictured her following closely behind, eyes wide open and overly helpful. Harry didn't reply but nodded and mumbled something unintelligible under his breath. Turning the pages of the file, he took out a photocopied rogues gallery of suspects. Each person had either a tick or a cross by their name.

"After chasing hundreds of leads and ruling out a random stranger attack, we nailed it down to these four people," he said. "One of them did it, but which one?" He sighed and sat back in his chair. At that moment, I felt empathy for him. His look was one of resignation, even defeat. The fact that he had not solved the crime weighed heavily on his mind. I sincerely hoped my help would provide the peace of mind he needed to get him back on the right track. At least he was here, and we were working together now.

The four people on Harry's suspect list were fascinating. Firstly, there was Jolene Hunter. She was to become Judith's mother-in-law in three months; beside her name was a big red tick. It was evident that she was high on Harry's list of possible suspects. Perhaps we should concentrate on her first.

"So, tell me about Jolene Hunter," I encouraged. "Why, in your opinion, is she such a good suspect?"

"She hated Judith with a passion," he declared. His tone was very matter-of-fact and authoritative. The statement shocked me. "Oh, in the beginning, she said all the right things. She said that she was truly sorry to hear of the girl's death and all that," he continued. "But as we began to ask more pertinent questions, her true nature showed itself. As it turns out, she was very jealous of Judith's talent in tennis. She saw it as a big complication, as Judith was a far better player than Rod, and Jolene feared that she would go much further in the sport. The family had put a lot of money and effort into getting him this far. Now they could see that he might give away his career to concentrate on helping Judith rise to the top of the rankings. Once Jolene got started on that subject, all the poisonous thoughts about her future daughter-in-law began to spill out. It was quite fascinating."

"I see that her son Rod is not on the list of suspects," I commented. "Were you able to rule him out completely?"

"Oh yes." His answer was firm and resolute. "Rod had an iron-clad alibi. He was in hospital at the time, having surgery on his ankle. This is why we could only get permission to search his bedroom. We were looking for the engagement ring."

"Yes." I agreed. "It appears to me that when you find the jewellery, you will uncover the identity of the killer. So, Don Hunter is Jolene's husband. What was he like?"

"Very aggressive and uncooperative. He's a successful lawyer in Manhattan. His nickname is *The Brick*. If you happen to face him in the courtroom, he'll hammer you so hard that you might want to plead guilty to get out from under his gaze. He's a bully. When we were arranging to interview Jolene, he made threats to ruin us all if we asked her certain questions. Well, that didn't go down well with us. So, we looked closer at his past. He has two convictions for second-degree assault and a couple of investigations into his financial dealings. To assuage him, we told him we suspected him of the murder and wanted to see what Jolene knew. Quickly, he backed down and offered to take a polygraph. Then, not wanting to be outdone, Jolene decided to take one as well." He smiled as he talked about it. "They both failed miserably. But as you probably know, a polygraph can't be used in court to prove guilt or innocence. Well, knowing that they both failed shook them up. They have been as quiet as a mouse since then."

I laughed.

"The arrogance," I chuckled. "They obviously thought that they could beat the polygraph. As a lawyer, Don should have known better, surely."

"We do see guilty people who are able to beat the polygraph," he said. "But it doesn't happen often. Our guys know what questions to ask and how to read the reactions. In the case of Jolene and Don

Hunter, we have no supporting evidence that will allow us to arrest them. We can't say that Jolene was even near the scene, and Don was in the courtroom at the time of the murder. This doesn't mean that he hasn't got information that we need. So, they both are high on my list anyway."

I nodded. Yes, we would look closer at them. There was something that didn't sound right with that couple. Then I picked up the third picture and studied the face of someone I had only heard about. He struck me as a sad and lonely individual. For a moment, I considered him, wondering what he had to do with Judith's murder.

"Franklin Evans," I breathed. "Why is he one of your suspects?"

"Oh, yes. Franklin was in love with Judith. He had been for many years. But she didn't feel the same way and had rejected him," Harry replied. "A peculiar guy. All his thoughts and sentences seemed to be garbled. I could hardly understand a word he was saying. Anyway, he wouldn't submit to a polygraph. So, we kept him under surveillance for a while. Nothing has come of it yet."

"He has a severe mental illness," I informed Harry. "It's unfortunate, but he probably thought that you were sneakily trying to invade his mind using electronic machines. Many with this illness who live in the community are a danger only to themselves. Yet there are those few who will attack others and even kill. So, I can understand your interest in Franklin as a suspect. We could leave him in the mix for the moment, though my gut feeling is that he had nothing to do with this murder." I advised. "Then again, I could be wrong. We'll see after we've looked at all the people concerned and the evidence." I placed Franklin's photo on the table and picked up the fourth picture. I was looking at a beautiful woman in her late twenties, with green eyes and red hair. Her name was Trisha MacLane. "Who is this woman?" I wanted to know.

"Ah, yes," Harry laughed. "Trish MacLane. Rod's ex-girlfriend. A very tricky young lady. She lied about many things during her interview. Then she failed the polygraph and flirted with all the detectives." He smiled to himself as he thought about their meeting.

"So, what's her story?" I wanted to know.

"She had several," he informed me. "One we were able to establish as definitely false. She told us that she had not seen Jolene for a couple of years. Well, we looked through the mall video tapes to see if Judith had been there. And guess who we saw having coffee together." He chuckled to himself as he recalled it.

"Jolene and Trish," was my suggestion.

"Yes," he confirmed. There they were, as bold as brass, laughing and chatting like old friends. But we never found any evidence that Judith was ever in the mall that day,"

"Don't these people know about CCTV?" I enquired.

"Oh yes," he chuckled. "But they have the strange idea that no one will ever see them on it."

"What a brain!" I exclaimed. And he laughed.

As we discussed these things, I realised how much pressure he felt to bring closure to grieving people. Yet he, too, was suffering. Memories of murder victims and scenes that he couldn't shake off were always with him; I knew that. I felt great compassion for him and wanted to help ease his pain.

"It must have been dreadful finding Judith in that condition," I commented. "I can't even imagine the images that you would have been confronted with."

He nodded and sighed heavily.

"Totally life-changing," he replied. "Once you've seen it, you can't unsee it. The image and everything that goes with it, changes you forever." His eyes were downcast, and I could feel the distress as he recalled each detail of that dreadful scene. He had witnessed Judith's half-naked, lifeless body, seen every stab wound, smelled the odour of decay and noted the disrespect of being discarded like trash. It was a disturbing graphic memory that would always be with him.

"Judith is healthy and happy now," I revealed. "She has no more pain or bad memories about that day. While I was in the heavenly place, Judith and I spent some time together. It was nice. She is a lovely woman." I didn't know whether Harry believed in God, Heaven, or spiritual things. Yet my instincts told me he needed to be nudged in that direction. As we discussed the case, I began to understand that he wasn't here merely to solve a murder. Harry was here to experience the healing of Heaven. "Judith is still a great tennis player and still plays to win," I said. "We had a game, if you can call it that. I had no chance against her. She knew exactly where to place that ball, so it was out of my reach, and she would win the point. I enjoyed my time with her." Then with some trepidation, hoping that I was relating my thoughts with clarity and sensitivity, I added, "I don't think she would want you to have those disturbing memories dominate your life. But she does want us to solve the mystery because it can be resolved. As a detective, having to deal with the devastating scenes and help heartbroken family and friends, perhaps you need a special touch from Heaven right here on earth."

Harry replied, "It is impossible to be unaffected by what we see and hear in our work. Yes, you are right. Most of the scenes we are called to are so horrific that I can't even talk about them. Then there are the bad people who cause so much devastation to unsuspecting families. We hear so many lies and excuses; it makes me mentally and emotionally tired. No matter how hard I try, I can't seem to get past it. Sleep doesn't come easy anymore." And he sighed heavily, but then he seemed to perk up. His eyes were alive and his back straight, strengthened with renewed interest in his investigation. "Okay, so when you talked with Judith, what did she say specifically about this murder?" He looked less anxious now as the tension drained out of his shoulder muscles, and he relaxed into the easy chair. I wondered if perhaps talking about his feelings had done some good.

"She told me that we must follow the science, matching it up with the evidence and look at the life and movements of every suspect that has already been questioned in the investigation."

"Sounds sensible to me," he laughed. "Well, perhaps we should get to it then," he suggested.

"Who's your best pick for the top prize and why," I wanted to know. "We'll start there and, if needs be, move on to the next if they are eliminated."

Harry picked up the picture of Jolene Hunter.

"This was the one who I think had the motive and the opportunity to do it. But I think she would have needed help. So, I can't rule out the others."

"Okay, we can start with Jolene. I'd like to see her interview."

Quickly, he put a pen drive into his computer, opened the file and there she was. At first, Jolene came across as a super-confident woman, able to hold her own in a serious conversation. She talked quite openly, even boldly, about how she had never approved of her son's choice to marry Judith. She and Rod had engaged in many heated discussions over the previous few months. Oh, she was sorrowful that Judith had been attacked and killed. But she felt that Judith had perhaps inadvertently put herself at risk. The interrogator asked her what she meant by that. Jolene wasn't phased. She told him that Judith didn't know her place in the family and expected Rod to follow her around while she rose in rank in the tennis world. The detective's interest peaks.

"What is her place?" he asks.

"Well, you know," she offered. "My son should be the main man. He shouldn't be following her around the world to boost her career. We paid good money so that he would have the chance to become number one in the tennis rankings. And he could be if it wasn't for her.'"

"So, tell me," said the interrogator, "Does Trish MacLane, who you had coffee with on the day of the murder, know her place in the family?"

Jolene's eyes widened, and I could tell she realised she had said too much. Awkwardly, she moved in her seat, pawing at her clothes and taking out a pendant to hold and look at. She did this without thinking.

"That is a very nice piece of jewellery," commented the interrogator. "A family heirloom?"

"A gift from my husband," she mumbled and hurriedly put the pendant back inside her clothes.

"What a brain," I chuckled as I realised what I had just seen. It was the missing Koru.

"I was just thinking that," he replied.

"What murderer takes the evidence of their guilt to their police interview?" And I couldn't stop giggling.

"Robbie," he said as he shook his head. "After all these years, I am not surprised at anything that goes on in that interview room."

Just then, we heard a knock at the door of the interview room. The door flew open, and Jolene's husband burst in. With great ardour, he demanded that they release his wife. So, they let her go due to a lack of evidence against her. This was the end of that interview.

"I'd like to see Trish MacLane's interview," I said. "Now, that will be fascinating. Let's see what she has to say."

So, Harry geared it up so we could watch. However, as it started, there was a knock at our front door, and Dad went to answer it. Harry paused the video, and soon, Dad brought Mike and Jeff in. They all sat down and relaxed.

"Has she figured it out yet?" Mike wanted to know. "I bet she has."

"Yep, she has," Harry replied. "We were just about to view another video because we think there may have been two people involved."

Briefly, I looked over at the picture on the screen. Suddenly, I was overcome with shock. I couldn't believe my eyes. Could I be seeing right? So, I looked a little closer.

"WOW! WOW! WOW!" I Breathed. "Look at that!"

"What?" the others wanted to know. And they all leaned in closer to look to see the video better.

"How stupid is that?!"

"Tell us what you see, Robbie," Harry pleaded.

"She's wearing Judith's earrings! Can you believe it?"

Harry enlarged the picture, focusing on the side of Trish's head and her earring. It looked to me like a Koru, but I knew that we would have to get Judith's mother to look at the picture to verify that it belonged to her daughter. Everyone was excited that I had picked that up. For the next few minutes, we discussed what would need to happen next. Because a lot of time had passed, a great deal more investigation needed to be done into the people concerned. We had only scratched the surface so far, but we had made a good beginning. Harry would be here for another couple of weeks, and we would be able to work on it more.

"Do you fancy coming on a trip to Auckland tomorrow?" asked Mike.

"Why??" I wanted to know. "The city is full of robbers and potential murderers. A dangerous place." Then I pretended not to care about going. In truth, I was very interested. I enjoy the banter between us. It's fun.

"You'll have a police guard," offered Jeff.

"With dogs and everything?"

"Well, we don't have a dog unit at the moment," said Mike. "But maybe I can borrow Poopsie from Mrs Jesson."

"Poopsie is a Pekingese dog with a pink bow in her hair," I informed Harry. "They spare no expense to catch the criminals in this Police Force. You can see why they need me, eh?" And we laughed.

"Poopsie is undercover," Mike mumbled, and he cleared his throat to sound serious. "I'm not supposed to tell you that."

"Okay," I chortled. "So, why are we going to Auckland tomorrow?"

"Chocco is going to appear in Court, and he and Joanne have asked if you would speak to the Judge on his behalf," said Mike.

"So, we thought we should first come and get the good word as to whether you are up to it or not," echoed Jeff.

"Oh, okay. I'll do it. You've convinced me," I replied. Then I turned to Harry. "Imagine the embarrassment of being replaced by a Pekingese princess with a pink bow in her hair. I couldn't ever live it down!"

"No," he commented with a wry smile. "Especially when her name is Poopsie."

CHAPTER FIFTEEN

The following day, we were up early. Chocco's Courtroom appointment was at 10am. Dad would take me, Harry and Eli in the van. Mike and Jeff would travel in their Police vehicle. There's nothing like a party, I say. Harry relaxed, taking in all the sights, while Eli talked to his social media friends, giving them a blow-by-blow account of where we were going and why. That was fun. As he does live broadcasts, we were all involved. He showed his online followers that I had survived and was on my way to speak to the judge on behalf of my attacker. I was pleased that he spoke of forgiveness with positivity and pointed out that moving forward in life to finding God's highest purpose, could be achieved. Yes, I certainly agreed with that.

As we arrived, I was pleased to see that there was disability parking near the entrance and access was well assured. Once inside, we were directed to a small office, and there we were greeted by a court officer who was specifically assigned to see that everything went smoothly. This was my first time in court, and I wondered what it would be like to be interviewed by a Judge. I was very excited.

We sat in the visitor's section of the courtroom, and others came and sat there as well. In all honesty, it looked like the Peanut Gallery, and I was tempted to giggle as I surveyed the people that had come to watch. They seemed such a motley crew. Nobody bothers to dress up in clean, nicely ironed city clothes these days. It was like they were just having a day at the beach. On the other hand, the people who worked at the court were beautifully dressed and stylish.

Chocco entered and sat at a table with his lawyer and his mother, Jo Anne. As I looked in their direction, my eyes widened with shock. Chocco's lawyer was none other than Chewing Gum Charlie, my old schoolmate! Wow, this was good news! He is an excellent lawyer, determined and thorough, and he takes good care of his clients. Yes, Chocco would be okay with him. I smiled as I remembered Chewing

Gum Charlie's tennis match with Larry the Larrikin. It was quite the talk of the town at the time.

I was very impressed by Chocco's appearance. He was well groomed, had cut and tidy hair, and wore a suit and tie. I hardly recognised him. He turned, looked over at me, waved and smiled. Quietly, he talked to his lawyer about what would be happening today as we all waited for the judge to appear.

Soon the court officer told everyone to stand. The door opened, and Judge Cedric Sharpe entered. He sat down at the bench and opened a file of papers. Looking around, he took note of who was here, resting his eyes on me for some moments.

"Case number 9000675WW," said the court officer. "We are here today to determine if Mr William Waimate should be held in custody until his trial. The charge is that on the day of March 20, 2020, Mr Waimate did commit grievous bodily harm with a knife on Miss Robin Mount and did wound her with the intent to steal goods that did not belong to him. The victim is in court today and has agreed to speak on Mr Waimate's behalf."

"Yes, I have heard that," replied the judge. "We will go through the usual procedure, and then I will talk with Miss Mount. Is Officer Mike Oliver in Court today?"

Mike stood up and walked briskly forward to the bench.

"Yes, Your Honour," he responded and stood to attention, waiting for further instructions from the judge.

"Do you still have that tennis match once a year in your town?" the judge enquired with a little chuckle. "I have heard about what happened last year. It's legendary. I must come to the next match. Who were those men that played?"

Mike laughed, and so did I.

"Oh, that was Chewing Gum Charlie and Larry the Larrikin," he informed the judge. "Yes, the whole town stopped for the entire afternoon. Next time, I'm bringing popcorn."

"Chewing Gum Charlie!!" exclaimed the judge. "Who's that?"

"Oh, that's me, Your Honour," said Chocco's lawyer. "I was robbed of that title last year," he explained. "Technically, I won. But some guy came onto the tennis court and gave my opponent a right hook to the jaw. Laid him out cold in front of us all. Apparently, Larry the Larrikin was fooling around with the guy's wife," he explained to the judge. "We were about to start the third set. I would have won. But I couldn't play him as he was. I was robbed," he bemoaned his loss.

The judge chortled to himself, yet he chose not to comment on that subject.

"So, back to the case at hand. Did this young man turn himself in on his own?" he asked Mike concerning Chocco.

"Yes, he did, Your Honour," Mike was pleased to tell him. "We had no idea who the perpetrator was until he and his mother turned up to check on Robbie at the hospital. But further to that, Robbie says that while unconscious, she went to a special place and was shown the magnitude of trouble the boy has had to cope with in his life. He apparently hasn't had an easy time. The defendant Chocco, as he is called, has displayed great remorse and a willingness to change his life. He has also said that he will make reparation to Robbie and her family, Your Honour."

"Good, good. We will discuss this in a minute," nodded the old judge. "But I want to check on something else first. I understand that Miss Mount is helping Police with another matter. It has come to my attention that a detective has travelled all the way from the United States to discuss the evidence in a murder inquiry and what she knows. Is this correct?"

"Yes, Your Honour. His name is Detective Harry Mann," replied Mike. "He's here in the Courtroom today."

"Good. I'd like to speak with him." The judge shuffled his papers as he waited for Harry to come forward. He then looked up and acknowledged Harry with a nod.

"Thank you, Detective, for coming," said the judge. "I understand that you have been conferring with Miss Mount about a cold case that you have had on your books for some years."

"Yes, Your Honour," confirmed Harry. "It seemed that while Miss Mount was unconscious, she talked to the woman who had been murdered and was sent back to solve the crime. I am a somewhat sceptical man, but when I heard some of the facts that she would not know but could relate, I discussed it with the Head of our department. Then as we were at a complete dead end and there was nowhere else to go, we decided to take a chance and talk to Miss Mount personally."

"Has she helped you so far?" asked the judge.

"Oh yes," Harry informed him. "We are thrilled with the results. I wired all the information Miss Mount provided to my colleagues in New York this morning. They have found the evidence we were looking for, and we now have three people in custody singing like canaries."

"Excellent," replied the Judge. "And how long have you been working with Miss Mount? I assume it must be a while."

"Only one day, Your Honour." Harry looked very amused as he relayed the facts to the elderly judge.

"One day?!" the judge exclaimed. Then he turned to his courtroom officer. "Write that down. We need her to work with us," he said. A ripple of laughter went through the courtroom, and people shuffled in their seats.

"Yes, Your Honour." And she giggled. The two policemen were dismissed, and now the judge wanted to speak with me. He asked that I come closer to his bench. So, I went and parked in front of him.

"I'd like you to tell me about the place that you visited while you were unconscious," he said. "What was it like? What did you see? What did you hear?"

"I first found myself in a huge library, Your Honour," I began. "Everything we say and do is written there. I saw several books, including an old family Heirloom Bible. I was able to see the history of the old book, meet the original owner and see the story of the lady who has it now. Her brother-in-law Mr Evans is in the courtroom this morning."

"So, he can verify that what you are telling me is correct?" said the judge.

Eli stood, and the judge indicated for him to come forward.

"Yes, I can, Your Honour," replied Eli. "I have known Robbie for less than a fortnight, and she has never met anyone else in my family."

The Judge then turned his attention back to me and told me to continue. And I knew that I must tell him the truth of what I knew about Chocco's life. He needed to know so that he could decide if the young man would be a threat to society.

"While I was in the Heavenly Kingdom, I was given a glimpse into Chocco's past, Your Honour. When he was only three years old, he was easy prey to the anger and violence of his stepfather. He was often happily playing with his toy tractor. However, this seemed to irritate his stepfather, who spent most of his time drinking alcohol. I watched as, one day, the man picked up the little boy and threw him against the wall. Chocco knew not to cry at this time, even if he was in pain, because worse would happen if he did. So, this was not the first time that this kind of violence had occurred. And this was the way his life was for close to twelve years. He and his mother have many scars, mentally, physically and emotionally and have found it difficult to escape from this man.

"On his seventh birthday, his wider family came together, and his uncle gave him a guitar. However, Chocco wasn't able to show his great pleasure and joy at receiving the gift. If he had done so, his stepfather would have taken it from him and smashed it right in front of him. This has been a way of life for this family. So, in order to keep the guitar, he and his mother were forced to hide it until it could be smuggled out of the house some time later. In all this mayhem, Chocco has remained loyal, obedient and caring towards both his mother and stepfather. He has never retaliated against the man who hurt him. Yet in the end, the pressure of living in that atmosphere of violence and pressure, never knowing what would be coming next, was too much, and he had no choice but to leave and make his own way in the world.

"While in the Heavenly Kingdom, I did meet the King. He had large nail prints in His wrists and in His feet. I also saw the tell-tale signs of where the soldiers had put the crown of thorns on His head. But the thing that affected me most was His great heart of love for people. He sees beyond what is, to what could be. And that is what He has done for both Chocco and I. He has given Chocco the gift of music and the ability to bring joy to many people. He has restored my life so that I could help solve the murder of Judith John and be here today to let you know that there is forgiveness for the greatest crime.

"This life here on earth has the elements of two halves, Your Honour. There is evil in the world. This can be seen in people who live only for themselves and don't care about their bad behaviours and hurting others. We all can get caught up in this mindset. It is an attitude that can become a permanent way of life. Yet, we were given a gift of hope in a man who, while He hung on a cross for crimes He did not commit, asked His father to forgive the people who had put Him there because they could not perceive the magnitude of their actions. Within all of us there is the ability to choose the better way. Not only do we have the written stories to guide us, but we also have a very near friend in the King to call on in times of trouble.

"Some people wonder that, if it was true that I actually went to Heaven where God lives, then why do I still have my disability? Well, Your Honour, my disability does not define who I am or what I can do. I am a unique person with gifts and abilities that only I can do. The same can be said for Chocco: he made a big mistake and did something awful. Yet, by the things he has done since the attack, he has already demonstrated that he is willing to change his ways and live a better life in the community. This is why I believe he is not a threat to society now, Your Honour."

"Thank you, Robbie," said the judge. "I really appreciate that you have come today. Very enlightening. We will adjourn for about fifteen minutes, and then I will issue my judgement."

Everyone stood, and the judge left the courtroom. Both Chocco and Chewing Gum Charlie came over to thank me for speaking to the judge. Charlie smiled at me mischievously.

"If there was ever anyone who could convince me that there was a God," he said. "It would be you. The things you said this morning were fantastic and very compelling. I was very proud of you. Thank you."

The lives of several people changed that day. Chocco didn't go to jail, and his mother, Jo Anne, received special help to rebuild her life differently. Detective Harry Mann was able to go fishing with Dad, Eli and Pastor Jon Ward. Initially, I thought it was a great idea. But now I hear that Pastor Jon wants to know every detail of my trip to the Heavenly Kingdom. Every detail??!! Time to disappear. Catch you on the flip side.

OTHER BOOKS BY TORIA NEWMAN

The Chrysalis – Robin's Story
2015, 2018, 2020 (revised edition due late 2022)

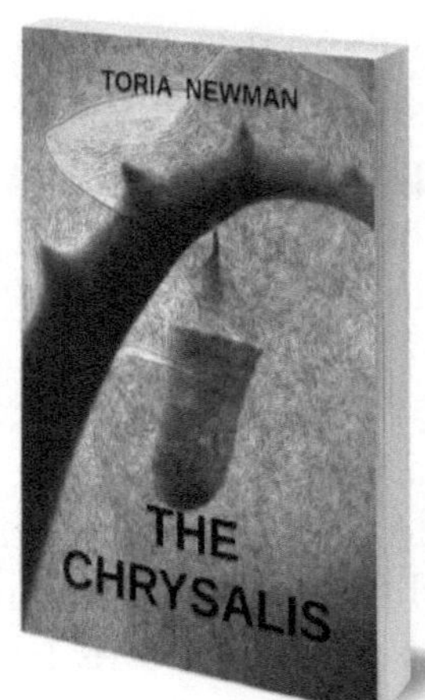

The Chrysalis is the first in a series of 3. Robbie is a young woman with Spastic Cerebral Palsy. She has limited speech and spends most of her time in her wheelchair. Robbie is involved in a tragic accident, and while unconscious, she visits Heaven. The Chrysalis is Robbie's journey from being like the caterpillar that feeds off the goodness of others, to where she becomes the chrysalis and discovers her own worth and abilities, becoming an adult. In the following two books, Robbie starts transforming into the beautiful woman she was meant to be.

Undercover – Miss Speedy Wheels
2020

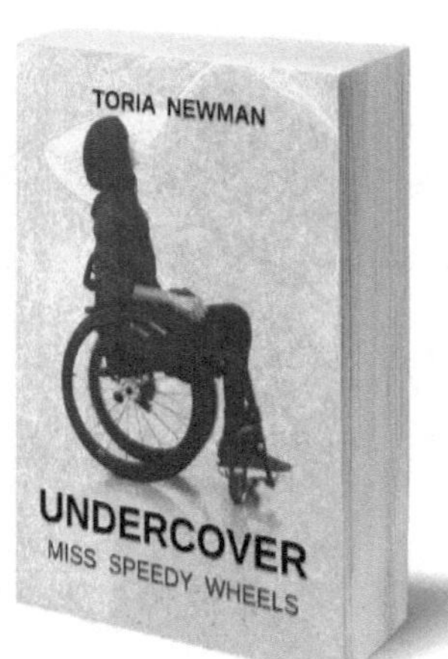

Undercover – Miss Speedy Wheels is the second book in the series of Robbie's life. Robbie starts to understand her worth in society, and the local Police have already found that she is a valuable asset to them. Robbie has other friends with similar disabilities, some of whom live independently and face various challenges. When one of them is murdered, Robbie takes on the task of helping her friends in trouble and assists the police in solving the murder. She takes great strides to reach her full potential on this journey of breaking out of the 'chrysalis'.

A Million Reasons

2019, 2020

A Million Reasons is Toria Newman's Autobiography living with Cerebral Palsy. Toria shares how she transitions from an institutional life in hospital to fitting into a family. Learning how to make her way in this world was very difficult for Toria, and she faced many twists and turns in her life's path. But when she put her life into the hands of her Creator, she soon found that there are many things that she can do despite her disability.

Toria Newman has her own website where
you can learn more about her.
Website:
www.toriasbooks.com
www.torianewman.com
Email: torianewman@xtra.co.nz